D0661427

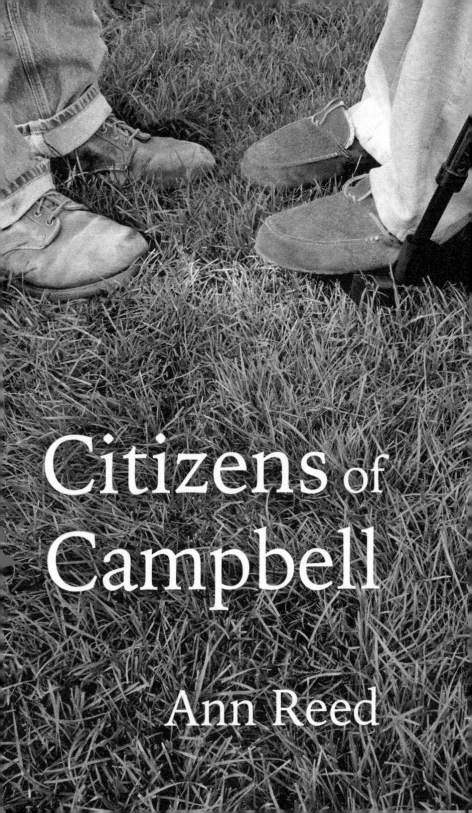

Citizens of Campbell

Ann Reed

ISBN: 978-0-9654862-0-0

Published by Turtlecub Productions
Minneapolis, MN

For Jane

Acknowledgments

I tend to work slowly.

But my friends will tell you that starting a novel at the beginning of the new millennium and finishing it in 2016 is a long time—even for me.

In January of 2000, while staying in a cabin near Spooner, Wisconsin, I wrote twenty pages of what would become this book, and then life happened. Over the course of the next thirteen years, I wrote about eighty songs, did some concerts and tended to my life.

My friend Marianne Norris moved to Los Angeles in 2013. Marianne had just retired from a career as a principal and associate superintendent in the Minneapolis Public Schools and was now ready to start something new. She was in the process of writing a novel. I offered to read it and provide some suggestions. Marianne said, "If I'm going to send you my writing, you have to send me something too."

I subsequently discovered the story I had begun thirteen years before. We sent pages back and forth, chatted on Skype twice a month, shared suggestions and encouragement. If it had not been for Marianne, I doubt I would have returned to finish what I started. I am grateful to her.

I was gently guided through the process of publishing by Gordon Thomas and Patti Frazee. Stevie Beck, copy editor, knows the book inside out. Gail Hartman kept me on track (and by that I mean held my hand) through the post-writing details. Kate Tucker offered her skills as a visual artist, but in the end steered me toward a photograph for the cover. Gail, Kate and I meet once a month to talk about and offer encouragement for all of our creative endeavors. I'm thankful for our little trio. Several friends read this before it was edited, and their comments were helpful and gracious. I hope you know what a blessing you are to me. I am beyond appreciative to all.

Thanks to Janet Mills, who took many photographs and patiently played with the cover until it felt just right. Thanks also to Doug Erickson and his son, Nathaniel, who can now add "model" to their résumés.

After forty years of being a songwriter, you'd think I would have no trouble finding the words to express my love and gratitude to my wife, Jane, who has been there for everything, all of it. Haven't found them yet. I'll keep working on that.

Citizens of Campbell

Ann Reed

When we think of friends, and call their faces out of the shadows, and their voices out of the echoes that faint along the corridors of memory, and do it without knowing why save that we love to do it, we content ourselves that that friendship is a Reality, and not a Fancy—that it is builded upon a rock, and not upon the sands that dissolve away with the ebbing tides and carry their monuments with them.

— Mark Twain,
in a letter to Mary Mason Fairbanks

If Earl Johansen had a nickel for every time he and Nearly Kelly got into trouble, he'd be living in one of those big, white, fancy houses instead of this tiny, pea-green, post-war box. He would be sitting at a large, round, maple table every morning. His steaming coffee would cool from the breeze moving the window curtains as if a tiny ghost were exhaling. The soft, sweet wind would carry the aroma of freshly mown grass and the sound of melodic bird song. In reality, the stench of the Karman's chicken-processing plant— the main employer in Campbell, Iowa—permeated as he heard his neighbor Al hacking and wheezing while trying to start his car.

Earl and Nearly weren't getting into too much trouble these days. They hadn't in a good long time.

Campbell was Earl's home, and most days he guessed he was

fine with that. He lived on Social Security and what money he had saved from years of diligent work as a janitor at the Teachers Credit Union and Campbell Savings and Trust. He had a small garden and a couple of window boxes. This year they held geraniums and impatiens he bought at the grocery store. These were attractive plants even when crowded together in tiny, black plastic containers on wide metal shelves outside the Hy-Vee. Earl's grandmother always told him that flowers could spruce up even the most tired-looking, dilapidated houses on the block.

To pay off their father's various debts after he died, Earl and his younger brother, Mitchell, sold the family home. It seemed that every time their father raised his hand to them, or came stumbling back in the dark, another section of paint would peel, another piece of wood would begin to rot. Earl enjoyed working with his hands and was knowledgeable about basic construction, plumbing and electrical work. Mitchell did some painting and contributed money to the effort. When they finished and the for-sale sign went up, the house was in better condition than it had ever been when they lived in it.

Soon after the war, a year before their father passed, their mother, Anna, ran off with Pastor Underwood, causing a scandal that this small town was still talking about. Anna had a flair for the dramatic and her exit from their lives, though unexpected, was done in true soap opera fashion, complete with a tear-stained note to her boys.

She named her boys after a character in a romance novel called *The Light Of Love*. The character's name was Earl Mitchell. Earl asked her once what would have happened if his brother had turned out to be a girl. "I would've named her Mitchell anyway," she said, "tell people it was a family name." In their genealogy, the family was riddled with names like Knudtsen, Sundqvist, Schmidt and Bauer, but no "Mitchells."

As far as Earl was concerned, Mitchell may as well have been a girl. His brother never wanted to play baseball or hang out with the guys from the neighborhood. He was either sensitive or a sissy, depending upon whether one was listening to their mother or their father.

Mitchell was odd. Even as a young boy, he was so neat that their room looked as if there were an invisible line down the middle. The left side, with clothes hanging out of drawers, a baseball glove on the floor, the closet floor a repository for dirty laundry, was Earl's. A typical teenage boy's haven, but a mother's housekeeping nightmare. The right side, a mother's dream: spotless and neat, books on bookshelves arranged according to size, shirts hung in the closet with great care by color and type, the bed carefully made every morning.

Mitchell lived in St. Paul now. He moved away and never looked back. At first, he wrote a few times a year, at Christmas, on Earl's birthday, and to relate the occasional interesting news item. The brothers attempted to talk on the phone but found they had little to say. Even Earl had a limit to how much small talk he could manage.

After Anna died, in 1965, Mitchell made more attempts to keep in touch with his brother. Earl found that he began to look forward to his precise handwriting on an envelope, and sometimes Earl sent clippings from the local paper about someone they both knew from their past.

In 1942, when Mitchell was a senior in high school, Nearly Kelly and Earl were recent graduates. They conspired to steal some of what they perceived to be Mitchell's sappy poetry and send it in to the newspaper for publication. The *Campbell Courier* had a section for "up-and-coming literary stars" that publisher Conrad Weigert had started in hopes of putting a little culture into the tiny paper amid all the news of war.

Earl knew where his brother kept his poems and the other drivel he was writing. He guessed that people in the town would tell Mitchell how great it was and then laugh as soon as the kid walked away. It would be a good joke. He never thought

4 – Ann Reed

Mitchell was serious about writing. Writers lived in New York, not Campbell, Iowa.

Much to Earl and Nearly's dismay the *Courier* never published the poems. Mr. Weigert had been so taken with them, he secretly sent them off to a contest in Des Moines called "The Corn Is Green." Before you could say John Keats, Mitchell had won fifty dollars and a writing scholarship to the University of Iowa in Iowa City.

Mitchell was furious when he found out what Earl and Nearly had done.

"The great irony," he said, red-faced and trembling with anger in front of his brother, "is that I now have to thank you. You and Nearly, by invading my privacy, have made it possible for me to get the hell out of here!"

Earl felt terrible, not only because he had taken something personal from him, but also because of the developing bruise under his brother's right eye, a gift tag that read: *from Dad.*

With World War II underway, Campbell felt small and isolated. Earl and Nearly figured that they had probably caused enough trouble at home and if they wanted some adventure, why not enlist before they were drafted? They could see the world, meet some new people and get paid to serve their country. It's not like they had any big plans.

****

The morning paper carried more proof of a world gone mad: articles about the nut job that bombed the Federal Building in Oklahoma City. And now, if you could believe it, a movie made from that poor excuse of a TV show *The Brady Bunch.* The mail contained bills, the usual advertising circular (*39¢ Good Guzzler Coffee at Kum & Go*) and a note from Mitchell. It was an article from the *Minneapolis Tribune* about Mitchell's writing career and his upcoming retirement from the University. A quickly penned note said: "Thought you might enjoy this." Mitchell had sent his book to Earl about a month ago. It sat on the kitchen table, gathering dust. According to the back of the book, it was about "coming of age and coming out in a small town ..." Earl tried to read it, but couldn't. Some things don't need to be shared. Especially with your older brother.

Back in February, he had received a letter from Mitchell:

> *Dear Earl,*
>
> *Thanks for your note. I'm sorry that Nearly is not well. I suppose we are in "that time of life," as Gramma Verna used to say. When we were young, I never quite knew what that meant. I do now.*
>
> *I don't have much news, but I did want to tell you that my agent is sending me out on a tour. I guess she heard about my upcoming retirement and is making sure I don't get bored! Part of it is to sell the book, of course, but some of the stops are lectures at colleges. It isn't confirmed yet, but the University of Iowa is on the list ...*

It was summer and no further word of an impending visit had arrived as yet. Perhaps that was just as well, Earl thought. Where would he stay? What would they talk about?

The results of the daily creaking contest between the door and Earl's knees revealed the door to still be the louder, and he was thankful for that. He sat on top of the three wooden steps he'd built for the very purpose of getting in and out of his faded green home. He took a pack of generic brand cigarettes (*$1.29 Smokes at the Kum & Go*) from the pocket of his plaid shirt, pulled one out and lit it with matches from O'Brien's Chinese Restaurant. He nodded at Al.

"Al," he said. It was a way of saying hello. Just the person's first name. Every man in Campbell knew how to say hello that way. Women, of course, said hello differently than men. They always had to say "How are you today, Mr. so-and-so" or "Good to see you, Mrs. what's-your-toes," accompanied by a brief hug or a touch on the arm. Why do they do that? Women were one of life's true mysteries. He figured that out early on and stopped trying to understand them. After a few steady girlfriends and a marriage that lasted all of five years with, luckily, no children, he decided he was better off alone. At seventy-one, his identity was simple: a citizen of Campbell, Iowa, a man who knew how to say hello to another man.

"Earl," Al replied, rubbing his unshaven chin and giving a glance up to the sky then back to the ground. He hacked, then added, "Gonna be a hot one."

"Hmm mmm," Earl nodded in agreement, taking another drag from his cigarette. Al walked around the car and opened the hood. Earl watched as Al went through his daily routine. First Al, then the engine coughing and choking. Al turned the key on his aged Dodge and then the AWWRURRUR-RURUR RURRU AWWRUR URURURRUURU sound as the spark plugs refused to spark and the engine stubbornly won another day of rest. Al stood scratching his head, looking at the engine as if perhaps today it would speak up and say, "It's the carburetor. It's the fuel pump."

Earl got up stiffly, adjusting his Cubs baseball cap as he started to walk toward the Veterans Home. Whenever he heard Al coughing like that, he considered quitting smoking. But probably not today.

He looked at the one-car garage painted the same color as his house. His 1982 Twilight Blue Chevy Caprice slept there. Three years ago he helped move Nearly into what would most likely be his last home. It was October and the days were shorter. Earl had stayed awhile, keeping Nearly company through dinner. Driving home in the dark from the VA, a dog crossed the road in front of him and Earl barely missed it, swerving, running the car up on the curb and into a lamppost.

Earl sat there, stunned. *I almost hit a dog*, he thought. *What if it had been a person? A kid?* Millie Aamodt came out of her house.

"You OK, Earl? My goodness. Don't move or anything. I

heard the noise and called the police. They should be here lickety-split."

Officer Dan Thompson sat on the curb with Earl, asking him if he was OK. Earl assured him he was.

"Just distracted, I guess." He told Dan about helping Nearly move into the home.

"Well, your insurance is gonna bump up a little, I expect," Dan said. "But there's a class you could take. It's offered once a quarter, sort of a ... a ... just to sharpen your skills."

Earl didn't say anything. He was too embarrassed.

"Seriously, Earl. Lots of our older folks are taking it to save money on their insurance."

In the end, Officer Dan Thompson let Earl go without issuing a ticket.

Lots of our older folks are taking it ...

Earl put the Caprice in the garage and closed the door.

Earl's gait was slow, partly because it was the way he did everything now but mostly because he wasn't in a big hurry to see Nearly in the home. He looked at the ground in front of him as he walked. The once chalky-colored sidewalk was almost brown from the history of rain, mud, hail and the shoes and bare feet of the young and old of Campbell. He noticed large cracks created by weeds that seemed harmless enough at first but had the strength and persistence to break cement. Earl remembered summer nights when he and Nearly snuck out of their houses and met behind the feed store on the corner of First and Broadway, two kids with little to do but create some trouble. Back then, Earl, who had seen Ruby Keeler in the movie *42nd Street*, thought it was stupid for a postage stamp-sized town like Campbell to have a street called "Broadway." He still thought it was stupid. But if they went and changed the name of the street now, three-quarters of the town would get so confused they'd be wandering around not knowing where they were or how to get home.

Their mischief was the kind practiced by boys for generations: frogs and other reptiles set free to work their magic with teachers and girls. When Earl and Nearly were in the lull of summer between sophomore and junior year, they got caught throwing firecrackers in front of Mayor Curly Neaton's horse Winnie. Winnie was pulling Curly, his wife, Dolores, and the Corn Queen, Miss Mary Jo Baillor, down Main Street during the tiny Fourth of July parade. The horse reared up and took off, the wagon sailing behind. The frightened mare galloped down Main then turned down First Avenue, not knowing where exactly she was going and not slowing down until Curly finally got hold of the reins. Winnie and the wagon ended up in Ole Sjordal's field, which was fine since Ole never did work that farm. The good people of Campbell put pressure on the mayor to punish these boys, make an example of them, and see to it that they learned a lesson. Curly decided to have the boys do something that would benefit the community, something his constituents could see and would remember come Election Day. Each day after school and for three hours on Saturday morning for two solid months, Earl and Nearly picked weeds that grew along the side of the road and threatened the smooth surface of the sidewalk.

Earl stopped on the corner of First and Main Street. Now, there was a good name for a street, he thought: Main Street. Solid and simple. In his youth, it was, indeed, the street that Campbell was built on and around. He looked up and saw the familiar shape of the civil defense speaker near the top of the telephone pole. Directly on top of this speaker was another one, about the same size but more square, dull with rust. Before Campbell entered the technological age, the warning announcements for civil defense or bad weather were made by the mayor from a small public works building adjacent to the town hall. It was a giant public address system, installed after the bombing of Pearl Harbor. The mayor never did get to issue an air raid warning, although they did have drills. Mostly, from this speaker, the populace was warned that tornadoes or severe storms were barreling in on them, and if they cared one whit about their lives they'd better take the appropriate action.

CITIZENS OF CAMPBELL! the mayor would boom, *THIS IS A TORNADO WARNING! BE PREPARED TO TAKE COVER!* Or: *CITIZENS OF CAMPBELL! GO DIRECTLY TO YOUR STORM CELLARS! THIS IS NOT A DRILL!*

Nowadays, when weather threatened, there was no mayoral announcement, just a loud, ugly-sounding siren. The bottom speaker was tested the first Wednesday of each month. The top speaker was left useless, old and silent.

****

Their first order of business after returning home from the war was a stop at Bob's Bar. Bob Hansen owned Bob's Bar and it was named by Bob and his wife, Roberta, who was also called Bob. Earl and Nearly sat atop the tall wooden barstools. They each enjoyed one boilermaker before switching to Budweiser.

"Keeeee-riiist!" Nearly said after emptying his fourth beer. "I sat on jeep seats more comfortable than this!" He lifted his left cheek off the stool and rubbed it.

Mr. Bob looked down the bar at the two uniformed men, jackets open, ties askew, but spoke only to Earl.

"Earl," he said, "don't you get sloppy on me now. I don't wanna have to throw you and that damned Eye-dee outta here."

Earl shook his head. *God, what an idiot.*

"Bob, jeez, he's not Italian."

"Yeah," Nearly said. "I'm an Indian. And I just got back from fighting for your sorry ass."

This was clearly the wrong thing to say. Mr. Bob was a little touchy about being classified 4-F and not being able to serve. During the war, much of the talk at the bar was Mr. Bob stating clearly what would happen if only BOB could go and fight. BOB would find that little weasel, Hitler. BOB would rid the world of Japs.

Mr. Bob threw the bar rag over his shoulder and took a few stiff steps toward the end of the long, polished oak bar where Earl and Nearly sat. Mr. Bob was not a small man. He was six feet four inches, broad-shouldered with one bad knee and two flat feet.

"What did you say?"

"Forget it, Bob. It's the beer talking," Earl said. Then, crushing out his smoke, he whispered to Nearly, "Finish it up and let's get out of here."

Approaching First Avenue on Main Street, Nearly looked up at the stars.

"Man, look at that." Nearly's eyes scanned the sky. "Ahh … Big Dipper … and Orion … and … big announcement speaker!" Nearly's face was pink with excitement. Or maybe just flushed with alcohol. "Earl! Let's go make an announcement," Nearly slurred excitedly.

"What? Are you drunk?" It was a rhetorical question.

"C'mon, man. We're home. I think we owe it to our town! A homecoming gift to these fine people. We got things to say!"

There was no denying that, to Earl, Nearly's idea made a certain amount of sense. They usually did. Of course, what makes sense at ten o'clock on a Saturday night after a liquid dinner and what makes sense at ten o'clock in the morning sober as a judge were two very different things.

****

The Veterans Home rested on several peaceful acres of land. While the lawns of the houses in the town were mostly speckled with brown, tired-looking grass, the expanse of green here was breathtaking. Even on the hottest of days, walking onto the grounds made the temperature feel as though it had instantly dropped ten degrees. From a short distance, the four large brick buildings seemed untouched by the ravages of weather and time, but on closer inspection, and once inside, it was clear they were as decrepit as the men who resided there.

The building Nearly lived in was called the "rehabilitation center." It was, in fact, a nursing home. About six or seven years after the war, Nearly was diagnosed with diabetes. He did not pay close attention to his disease and a few years ago ended up losing part of his right foot. Diabetes, COPD, years of nutritional neglect—difficult to say what might get a man in the end.

Earl walked into the center and, out of habit, removed his cap and smoothed what was left of his hair. The decaying smell was a familiar greeting along with the walls, which had been painted a tired, pale shade that couldn't quite find the energy to be sky blue or robin's-egg blue. He walked down the hall. A few men sat in their wheelchairs outside of their rooms, staring into space. As he passed, one of the old soldiers, with all the strength he could muster, said: "Sir! Sir! Yes, SIR!" Earl looked at him.

"Are you talking to me?" Earl said.

"Sergeant, I am talking to you, sir!" If this guy weighed a hundred pounds, Earl would have been surprised.

"I'm … uh … sorry?" Earl said uncomfortably.

"Yes, sir. Move along." Earl did as he was told. As he walked down the hall, he offered a short prayer, asking please, before he resembled any of these guys, to be carried out feet first.

Earl peeked into Nearly's room. He heard a rattling snore coming from Nearly's roommate, Carl, but Nearly was not there. As Earl wandered farther down the hall, he heard the hissing of nebulizers, a baseball game blaring from a radio, a nurse trying to communicate with a patient: "NO, MR. DIETRICH, I'M NOT YOUR WIFE. I'M YOUR NURSE."

Sunlight poured over the faded yellow walls of the day room, shedding light on the mismatched furniture. There were 1950s couches, faux leather chairs and heavy wooden tables with cigarette burns dating back to when the patients were allowed to smoke inside.

In front of the television, in a wheelchair, sat Nearly. His hair, still plentiful, was black with a smattering of gray that sparkled in the sun. His chin rested on his chest, rising and falling with each shallow breath. Across his lap was a small quilt that had accompanied Nearly since the VA became his address. The game show *The Price Is Right* hollered, "C'MON DOWN!"

"Nearly …" Earl said. "Hey … Nearly …"

Nearly's head popped up. He had an oxygen tube in his nose, the tank attached to his chair.

"Earl. Hey. I was hopin' you'd show up." Nearly's speech was slow. He looked as if he had shrunk. That's what people do here, Earl thought: they keep shrinking until they're gone. His friend's eyes were dull. He looked pale. It seemed the only time the man got outside was when Earl came to visit.

"So," Earl said, taking a seat, "how's it goin'?"

"Well …" Nearly said slowly, "it goes, I guess."

The gaps of silence were familiar to the two friends. Even as kids, they didn't feel the need to fill up every minute with chatter.

"You got a smoke for me?" Nearly asked.

"Well, Nearly," Earl replied carefully, eyeing the oxygen tank, "seems like you got some oxygen there." Nearly looked at him blankly.

"So?" Nearly finally said.

"Don't you think it's a little dangerous? I mean with the oxygen and all."

"Nah."

"I don't really want to be blown to kingdom come. Tell you what—let's go outside anyway. It's a real nice day out there."

As Earl wheeled Nearly down the hall, Nearly announced his destination to every nurse that passed.

"Goin' for a smoke …"

His voice was most likely too soft for anyone to hear as they rolled by. One nurse, the one Nearly referred to as Wilma after one of his favorite cartoon characters, Wilma Flintstone, made a disapproving face whenever the two men made a beeline for the door. Her red hair was piled on her head, her features sharp enough to cut paper.

The first few times Earl took Nearly out for a cigarette, she stopped them.

"Where are you taking this man?" she had asked Earl.

"Goin' for a smoke," Nearly answered. The nurse directed her comments at Earl.

"You *do* know that we frown upon our patients smoking," Wilma said. Earl was about to reply when Nearly took the words out of his mouth.

"Gonna die anyway."

After a month of Earl visiting almost every day, she let them go by without stopping them, her disdain clearly etched in her expression. This time, however, she blocked their way.

"Excuse me," Wilma said. "I really cannot allow this man to smoke. It endangers him and everyone around him. Have you not noticed the oxygen tube?"

"He's not going to smoke," Earl said. "You have my word. We're just going to sit outside."

Wilma pursed her lips, looking squarely at Earl, and proclaimed, "I will have an aide keep an eye on you."

Earl hit the handicap button and the heavy metal door swung open. "Honest to God, Nearly, it's like we're twelve years old."

"Yup," Nearly said. "Gimme a smoke, Joe."

Earl parked the wheelchair next to a bench on the lawn.

"I can't, Nearly. And believe me, I'd love to have one too."

Nearly looked at his friend. "You aren't gonna give me a smoke?"

"No, I'm not." He glanced over at the entrance where a large, blond man who looked like he might play fullback for the Vikings stood, his arms crossed over his barrel chest.

Nearly narrowed his dark eyes. "Huh. Pullin' out on me."

"Oh, for cryin' out loud, Nearly. Do you know what happens when you got oxygen and a match?"

Nearly thought for a minute.

Perhaps Nearly was having a war memory. Perhaps he was recalling the suspension he got for the small explosion in Miss Davies science class. Miss Davies thought she was the only one with matches. She was not.

"Boom," he meekly replied.

"That's right," Earl said. "Boom."

They sat for a couple of minutes. Nearly reached into his pocket and pulled out a small tin of mints. He popped one in his mouth, returned the tin to his pocket, closed his eyes and lifted his face to the sun.

"This is the second time," he said at last.

"Second time for what?" Earl asked.

"Second time you wouldn't do somethin' with me. All these years."

"I don't think that's such a bad record," Earl said. "What was the first time?"

"'Member when we got home? I wanted to go and make an announcement over the PA. We got to that public works building at the town hall and you wouldn't do it."

"Well I just didn't feel like getting arrested my first night back home!" Earl said.

"Yeah," Nearly said, a chuckle escaping, followed by a cough. "Y'know what?"

Earl didn't say anything. He knew Nearly was going to tell him anyway.

"That's my one big disappointment. No kidding."

"Oh, come on," Earl said.

"No, really. If I could've been on that PA, everyone in town would've listened to me for once."

Nearly was the product of a woman who was Chippewa and a man whose idea of a long-term relationship was anything lasting shy of two weeks. He had a photograph of the man his mother told him was his father. He looked like Nearly—short and stocky, with a fleshy face highlighted by dark eyes and a full head of dark hair. When his mother was pregnant with him, she fell in love with a man named Sean Kelly, a man who didn't care if she was an Indian—a rare find, someone who wanted to marry her and raise the child she was carrying. He died in an automobile accident on County Road 12 two days before the wedding.

Most of the people of Campbell were not outwardly hostile to Nearly or his mother; they simply chose to ignore them and talk about them behind their backs. It pissed Earl off to hear the gossip and endure the bigotry, especially from his own father. As a boy, when he brought Nearly home for dinner, he would embarrass Earl by saying, "Well, here's the chief. How's everything at the reservation?"

In school, a teacher openly humiliated Nearly by telling him that he might be better off leaving school and finding a job because she knew that education was not a value "his people" held. When Nearly graduated, he placed a shirt covered with skunk in her office and closed the door.

"What would you say?" Earl didn't know why he was even asking.

"Huh?"

"If you got to the PA. What would you say?" Earl repeated.

"Hmmm," Nearly said, his brow furrowed. "I guess I'll have to think about that one."

After a few minutes, Earl thought Nearly had fallen asleep. Looking around the grounds, he saw a resident in a wheelchair sitting outside the door, smoking. The man looked familiar. Earl stood up to begin pushing the wheelchair toward the building to perhaps get a better look at the guy, when Nearly spoke.

"Hey. Is Al still trying to start his car? You didn't give me the Al report."

Earl sat down. "Yup. Still trying."

The two men sat outside for an hour, their conversation wandering.

"What'cha do last night, anyway?" Nearly asked.

"Not much. Watched *The Great Escape*."

"That's a good one. Steve McQueen. How many times have you watched that?"

"No idea," Earl said. The truth was, he only owned six videos and they all seemed to be about the war: *The Great Escape, The Longest Day, Mister Roberts* and a couple of other bloodless depictions of the Allies defeating the enemy.

When Earl finally pushed Nearly back inside, he said, "Where to?"

"My room, I guess. I'm kinda tired."

"You want me to help you get into bed?" Earl offered.

"Nah, that's OK. Just get Wilma to help me. My good foot is a little swelled up."

As Earl left, returning to the caress of the warm summer day, his throat burned and he found himself as close to weeping as he had been in a very long time.

After leaving the VA, Earl stopped at the Hy-Vee to get a couple of TV dinners, a head of lettuce, a cucumber and some Sara Lee pecan coffee cake. As he headed down the produce aisle, he saw Marlene Goodhue thumping muskmelons. He had one or two dates with Marlene in high school. At seventy, she was still a very attractive woman, slim with an air of lightness about her, as if gravity wasn't pulling on her quite the way it pulled on everyone else. After high school, she went to the University of Minnesota and lived in St. Paul until her father became ill and she returned to Campbell to care for him. Earl knew he'd died ten years ago and that Marlene had decided to stay in town. Earl seemed to remember that she had a degree in horticulture or some advanced gardening degree. She had always been smart and plants seemed to trust her.

"Well, Earl! Hi!" she said, hugging him briefly. Earl accepted the hug tentatively, patting her lightly on her back. He didn't really like to hug people, but Marlene seemed to want one.

"Hey there, Marlene," Earl said, forgetting he was speaking to a woman and not Al or Nearly. "So … picking out a melon?" *My God, what a stupid thing to say.*

"I'm having some ladies over for bridge tonight," she volunteered, nodding at the fruit in her cart. "How are you?" she asked with great concern. With most people, "How are you?" is a disposable phrase. Coming from Marlene, it felt genuine.

"Not bad. Pretty much the same, I guess."

"Uh-huh," she responded. There was a squirmy silence. Earl felt he had to say something. Anything.

"I was just at the VA visiting Nearly."

"Oh," Marlene said with a touch of sadness. "How is he doing?"

"Oh, not so good, I don't think. He's still Nearly though."

Marlene's laugh in response was quiet and kind.

"You two were always up to something. I'll bet this is hard for you."

Earl looked at his feet. He felt like saying, *Don't you get tired of getting older? Don't you just hate watching your friends and people you know die one by one? I do. It stinks.*

What he did say was: "Well, yes. I guess so."

Silence again. Earl was about to nod and make his escape when Marlene said, "Listen. My grandniece, Laurie, is coming to visit next week. Would you like to have a good, home-cooked meal with us?"

"Oh. Gee, Marlene," Earl said with an apologetic smile. "That's nice of you, but you don't have to do that." Actually, the "home-cooked" part sounded pretty good. He didn't know about having to make conversation, especially with a child.

"I don't *have* to, I want to! It's no trouble," Marlene said. "You're in the Campbell phone book, right? And really, I've been meaning to do this for a long time. I'll call you."

In most cases, "I'll call you" means: you're pretty much off the hook and I didn't really want to do this either. But Earl had the feeling that Marlene was good for her word.

****

The next day was a repeat of the previous one. Earl and Nearly sat outside after having the same conversation about why Nearly could not have a cigarette.

"I'll give you a million dollars if you give me a stick," Nearly said.

"You don't have a million dollars," Earl said.

"Yes, I do." Nearly nodded lightly, tugging the quilt across his lap. His face came close to displaying his once-famous grin.

"Guess who I ran into at the Hy-Vee?" Earl said after a moment.

"Where?" Nearly looked confused.

"The Hy-Vee. The grocery store."

"You mean Carson's." It wasn't a question. Earl was puzzled. Didn't Nearly remember that Carson's went out of business fifteen years ago?

"Whatever. Guess who I ran into?"

"Can't imagine," Nearly said, his voice tired.

"Marlene Goodhue."

"Marlene …" For a minute, Earl was afraid that his friend didn't remember her.

"You used to be pretty sweet on her. She still single?"

"Ancient history. She said she might call and invite me for dinner."

"That's good. Man cannot live by TV dinner alone …" Nearly's voice trailed off.

The wind came up suddenly and a few acorns dropped from the large oak tree.

"Trees," Nearly said suddenly.

"What?"

"'Trees.' 'I think that I shall never see a poem lovely as a tree.' By Joyce … Joyce what's-her-name."

"Kilmer. Joyce Kilmer." Earl paused for a moment and looked at Nearly, who was nodding. Then Earl added, "Who was a guy, by the way."

Nearly looked up at the oak umbrella. "Doesn't matter. I like Mark Twain more than poetry guys but he … she … was right, trees are better."

The following Tuesday evening, with his thirteen-inch color television sitting across the gray Formica table from him like an electronic friend, Earl ate his Hungry-Man TV dinner—turkey, mashed potatoes, peas and some kind of strange cobbler thing that was red, gooey and sweet. Before Nearly became ill and entered the home, the two men would dine together at least twice a week. Nearly preferred Banquet over Swanson's and pork or roast beef over turkey.

Earl was watching *Wheel of Fortune*. Vanna was wearing a very attractive dress, with one shoulder bared. Earl thought that Vanna was beautiful but suspected that she was not the brightest bulb in the house. He secretly hoped that Vanna had a degree in physics or something, that she could do more than just turn letters and look pretty. He respected women who were smart. Like Marlene.

The phone rang. Earl thought it would be too strange if it was Marlene on the other end, calling just when he'd been thinking of her. It wasn't and, to his surprise, he felt a little disappointed. The voice on the other end was Lenny Gustafson. Lenny went from high school to working in the chicken-processing plant and had been there for forty-five years. Most Wednesday nights, Earl would run into him at the tavern and they'd shoot a game of pool.

"Earl!" Lenny said his name as if he'd just recognized him.

"Lenny," Earl said.

"Hey. Listen. Betty's outta town visiting her sister and I was thinkin' maybe you wanted to have a burger and a game of pool."

"Oh, well … thanks. I'm just finishing my dinner here, Lenny." Earl would be seeing Lenny tomorrow night. Two nights in a row of Lenny's chatter would be too much. Besides, after dinner, he wanted to do the crossword puzzle and then do some reading before he went to bed—mysteries, mostly, some Zane Grey, an occasional book on the war. It was a way to pass the time. He was reading a book right now that made him laugh out loud. It was *Tales of the City* by a guy named Armistead Maupin. The librarian had recommended it when he asked for something with a little humor. He wondered if Mitchell knew this guy. It made him think about actually giving Mitchell's book a try.

"You watchin' The Wheel?" Lenny asked.

"Yup."

"Boy, that Vanna …" said Lenny, a leer crawling across the phone line. Earl hated the way some men talked about women. His grandmother had taught him to respect women, and he still felt that some thoughts men harbored were better kept unsaid.

"Yes … well … anyway …" Earl said.

"Yah. OK. Well, maybe I'll see you tomorrow, then," Lenny said.

"OK. Good."

"Hey!" Lenny said almost as an afterthought, "How's ol' Nearly doin'?"

"He's deteriorating a little but about the same, I guess, Lenny."

The next day, when Earl told Nearly that Lenny had asked about him, Nearly said, "You didn't tell him to come visit me, did you?"

"No, I didn't. Did you want me to? I didn't think you really liked Lenny."

"No! Jeez, no," Nearly said, as animated as Earl had seen him lately. One of Nearly's many jobs in town was working in the chicken factory with Lenny. "That guy's so dumb he couldn't pour piss out of a boot if the instructions were written on the sole. You can tell him I said so."

****

Early Thursday morning, Earl was washing the week's worth of dishes. He usually waited until there were at least four plates and a fistful of silverware. Otherwise, it was a waste of water. The telephone startled him and a fork flew into the soapy water, splashing suds on his face. Grabbing a dish towel, he wiped his hands and, flopping the dish towel over his shoulder, picked up the phone.

"Hello?" he said pleasantly.

"Earl? It's Marlene." Her voice sounded like spring.

"Well, what a surprise. Hello!" Earl hoped he didn't sound too pleased to hear her voice.

"I told you I'd call."

"Yes ... yes, you did." Lots of people say they'll call, but they never do, he thought. I'll bet there are men in that place with Nearly with enough IOUs for visits and calls to fill up Wrigley Field.

"Are you free to have supper with us on Sunday?"

Earl had been thinking about his response for a few days now. Just in case.

"I would love to, Marlene. Thank you for the invitation." There. He'd said it. And in a very gentlemanly way too. His grandmother would've been proud.

"How about six o'clock? Would that be all right?" she asked. Earl agreed and after a few pleasantries, hung up the phone. Then he sat down and wiped sweat off his brow with the dish towel.

The dinner invitation occupied Earl's thoughts as he walked to the VA. He felt good one minute and terrified the next. What if they ran out of things to say? What if he embarrassed himself?

"So ... you got a date, huh?" Nearly said.

"It is not a date!" Earl said, a little too defensively. They were sitting in the day room. It was a gloomy day, and the rain ticked the windows as it steadily fell.

"Are you gonna wear your good flannel shirt?" Nearly teased. Earl looked at his feet and tried not to smile. The fact was, Earl had spent a considerable amount of time pondering what he should wear. He couldn't remember the last time he was invited to eat at somebody's home. He didn't think his daily "uniform"— worn flannel shirt and blue jeans—would be appropriate, no matter how clean they were. He decided on a crisp, blue cotton long-sleeved shirt and a pair of khakis.

"You bringin' anything?"

"What do you mean? She's cooking." Earl tensed.

"Well, according to Miss Manners, you're supposed to bring something."

"Like what? And since when do you know anything about Miss Manners?"

"She was on the TV. *Oprah*."

Earl felt panic creeping up his back like a lost ant patrol.

"OK, smarty. Tell me what to bring."

Nearly thought a minute. A light hiss came from the oxygen tube. His voice was so soft; it was as if he were talking to himself. He rubbed his chin and said thoughtfully, "Can't really bring wine anymore ... never know if people have, y'know, been through rehab or something. So, I guess ... oh ..." he lifted his head a little and smiled, "maybe flowers."

Earl didn't tell him so, but he was grateful for the tip. There was no florist in Campbell anymore. Rose Floral went the way of Carson's Grocery. He remembered the plants and flowers at the Hy-Vee. They were brought in from Zeel's florist in Pella, wrapped in starchy cellophane. He would stop there on his way to Marlene's on Sunday.

****

Verna Sorenson looked at the man her daughter was going to marry and knew she was looking at what her own mother would have called Beelzebub. Jack Johansen was attractive as hell, which made sense since that's most likely where he came from. She talked with her daughter, begged Anna to reconsider, take some time, but it was no use. Lust, she thought. Verna did her best to stay out of her daughter's business. "You're a grown woman now," she told her daughter on her wedding day, "and you make your own decisions." She carried the sad, heavy knowledge in her heart that her daughter, in spite of Verna's best efforts, was selfish, impulsive and sorely lacking common sense.

Verna tried living her life by the Ten Commandments but could never remember all of them. Besides, her father was a drunken, violent man and she didn't think God really wanted her to honor him. Not surprisingly, she married a man who turned out to be a younger version of her father. No, the Ten Commandments did not work for her. Once she began to live her life by the seven deadly sins and the seven heavenly virtues, things made a bit more sense. They were a better measure.

Anger. The first time Verna saw bruises and welts on her grandsons she thought the top of her head might come off. Thinking that it might have been an isolated incident, she stayed quiet. When it became clear that Jack was repeatedly hitting the boys—and her daughter—she could not stay silent.

It was Christmas Eve 1936. Earl was twelve years old. Mitchell was eleven, and on his upper left arm was the shape of a multicolored hand. Verna went into the kitchen to help Anna with dinner.

"Would you ask Jack to come in for a moment?" Verna said, not looking at her daughter. "I have a gift and I'd like to give it to him in private."

"You have a … gift? For Jack?" Anna was surprised. As she walked out of the kitchen she took a long look back at her mother who, basting a turkey, was softly humming.

Jack walked in a few minutes later. He was no longer the tall, lean, well-muscled man Anna married thirteen years ago. The paunch in his midsection seemed to have taken a couple of inches off of his height. Sloth.

"Goddamn!" Jack exclaimed as he walked in, "This smells great! I'm starvin'!" He did a long inhale and patted his stomach. Gluttony, Verna thought. And at a time when most folks had so little. Thank

god for living in a close community where people looked out for one another.

He sat down with a grunt and with his hands on his knees, leaned forward and said, "Anna says you got me a present!" Greed, *thought Verna.*

"No, I don't," Verna said honestly. "I wanted to talk to you. Alone."

Jack leaned back and looked at Verna. His face went from happy to wary in the blink of an eye. "What do you want?" he said.

"I want you to stop harming my daughter and her children." Verna folded her arms over her ample chest and stood in front of him like an oak tree.

A spitting laugh escaped his mouth.

"Her children?" He stood up. Verna didn't move. She was five feet three inches tall. Jack was six feet one inch. He stood toe to toe with her, looked down on her and said quietly, "They get what they deserve. It's none of your business, old woman."

Verna raised her head to look at him and made sure she looked him in the eyes. "If I see one more bruise on Earl or Mitchell or Anna," she began.

"You'll what?" He said in a teasing voice. "You'll what?"

Her eyes burned into his as she said, "I ... will ... come ... for ... you. I will make sure you never have another peaceful moment. I will take a carving knife and take away your manhood."

At this, Jack moved his head back slightly, and when he did his torso moved back as well. His lips parted.

"I ...will ... do it." She continued slowly, firmly. "Do you know how my husband died? Do you? Has Anna ever told you? Perhaps you should find out." She unfolded her arms, calmly turned around and took the carving knife from the counter. She took a long look at it. Then she looked at him. She hummed "Joy to the World."

****

Marlene lived not far from the VA in the small, solid house

where she and her sister, Muriel, were born. She had not planned to return to her family home. Very few people do. But life happens and plans change.

At the dawn of the 1980s, she was looking forward to retirement, simultaneously a little way off yet tantalizingly close. Marlene was fifty-five; her partner, Jeanne, was sixty-two. They had been careful with their money, investing and living a simple, frugal, happy life, taking a trip each year but never anywhere remotely exotic. One of their favorite places to go was either Anderson's or Fenstad's resorts up near Grand Marais, Minnesota, on the north shore of Lake Superior.

When Jeanne was diagnosed with cervical cancer a year into the new decade, Marlene sat by her during chemo treatments, telling her, "You'll come through this and when you do—we will go wherever you want to go. Anywhere in the world. Adventure time. Screw the money." Some days Jeanne would just smile. On better days, when she had some energy and wasn't feeling so nauseated, they would look at maps and catalogs of hikes in Europe and Asia, sailing in Greece.

One day, after Jeanne had been admitted to the hospital to take care of another infection, it was discovered that the cancer had spread. Marlene climbed into the hospital bed with her beloved. She once again said, "Wherever you want to go …" and Jeanne replied, "I want to go home."

Two weeks after Jeanne's memorial service, Marlene got a phone call from Helen Watkins, her father's next-door neighbor in Campbell.

"Listen, I hate to bother you up there but Jimmy Stern found your dad wandering around downtown this morning wearing nothin' but his boxers. I got your number from the emergency card on his refrigerator. I hope you don't mind."

The emergency card—and a key for Helen—was something Marlene's sister, Muriel, had decided upon after their father had a minor heart attack three years earlier. Muriel put Marlene's name first. When Marlene protested, Muriel said, "You're closer! I'm way the heck back in Phoenix!"

Marlene moved through those days as if she wore a lead apron. Driving several times from St. Paul to Campbell and back gave her time to think. Everywhere she looked in the Twin Cities, sadness pushed on the walls of her heart as she saw the places where she and Jeanne had walked, met friends and danced. Perhaps moving back to Campbell might help it ache a little less.

Her father had a quick decline and died, leaving the house to his two daughters. After the funeral, when all of the friends, neighbors and relatives were sent on their way, the two sisters sat, exhausted. After several toasts to their father with a Glenlivet on the rocks (his favorite), Muriel said, "Take the house."

"What? Muriel, you must be drunk."

"Nope. Well, yes, a little. Not used to scotch, I guess, but … take the house. You sure earned it."

"Mur …" Marlene began to protest.

"Look, I could've come and helped these past couple of years. I could've. But I didn't. I showed up … what … twice? Three times? And there you were, having just lost Jeanne and then saddled with some demented old man who thought you were Verna Sorenson." With mock solemnity, Muriel raised her glass, "To Verna Sorenson. Whoever she is, she calmed the old man down."

Marlene laughed. It had been a long time since she and her sister drank together. "Verna Sorenson was Earl Johansen's grandmother …" For some reason, this set the women off on a laughing jag.

"Earl … Johansen … his grandmother …" Muriel was laughing. "How did dad …"

"Don't … know …" Marlene was laughing so hard, tears ran down her face. When the first tear dropped on her hand, the rest that followed were filled with sorrow and loss.

"I … I'm sorry … I'm sorry … I …"

"Oh, honey, c'mere …" Muriel said and hugged her sister. "Too much. Too much. It's small comfort, I know, but you have me."

Sunday the skies were streaked with gauzy sheets of clouds. They floated over Campbell on their way eastward to Illinois and beyond. Earl looked to the west, a habit he picked up from his grandmother.

"That's where the weather comes from, over there." Verna would say. "Always look—you can see it coming and you'll always be ready."

They could use some more rain, Earl thought as he walked to the Hy-Vee. A good soaking rain. There was, according to the weatherman on the TV, a "chance" of rain this evening but a "better chance" on Monday.

There were flowers in the flower stand that didn't look like any color he had ever seen in nature. Marlene would know a false flower, he was sure of that. He chose a bouquet with white and red carnations, two yellow sunflowers and some other small but pretty flowers that he couldn't identify. Simple is best, he thought. On the way to the checkout, he passed the bakery. Pearl Sturner stood behind the counter, putting things away, preparing to go home. Earl was hoping she didn't see him. Without question, Pearl knew her baked goods. Whenever there was a bake sale to raise money for a school trip or other community project, Pearl's cookies, pies and cakes were snapped up immediately. Also undisputed was the fact that she was the biggest gossip in Marion County. If you ever wanted word to get out, everyone knew: Telephone, telegraph, tell Pearl.

"Hey, Earl!" Pearl called out. "You look nice. Hardly ever see you without your hat! What's the occasion?" Her words came out rapidly, earnest and harmless enough, but he knew she was fishing.

"Oh … hi, Pearl. I didn't see you there."

"Just getting ready to close up—need anything? It's half-price. I was just gonna box stuff up and run it over to the guys at the home. Where you off to?"

What the hell, thought Earl. *She's going to find out anyway.*

"I'm having supper over at Marlene Goodhue's. I ran into her here and I guess she's taking pity on me." Earl gave a little chuckle. Pearl didn't even give him a courtesy laugh.

"That's nice!" she chirped. "Funny she's invited a man over, I mean … I thought she was… hey! You need dessert!"

"No, really, thanks for thinking of it but …"

"I insist," Pearl said. "Now, let's see … that Marlene … I don't think she's much into sweets and God knows a man doesn't want to walk into a lady's home with a cake … no, siree. Oh, here we go …" Pearl bent down and when her head popped back up, she set a small, round tart on the counter. It was a thing of beauty, custard in some light pastry topped with fresh, sliced strawberries, plump blueberries and several large raspberries in the middle. "For you, I'll mark it down even more. I mean, how often do you get asked over to a lady's house?"

With a bag containing the tart, and the flowers poking out of the top, Earl walked to Marlene's. He tried to rid himself of the knowledge that, thanks to Pearl, the entire town would be informed of his dinner invitation before he had taken one bite of supper.

****

A beautiful array of perennials and flowering shrubs graced the front of Marlene's home. Even in the heart of summer, there wasn't a spindly plant among them, not one flower that needed to be deadheaded. Reds, blues and yellows in a variety of shades greeted every visitor. Looking down at his flowers wrapped in cellophane, Earl was beginning to lose what small amount of confidence he had when Marlene answered the door. She gave Earl a light hug as he crossed the threshold.

"I'm so glad you could come!" she exclaimed. "What a beautiful evening!"

"Yes, it sure is," Earl said. "I know you have a lot of flowers but … well … here …" he said, offering the bouquet.

"How lovely. Thank you."

"You hardly need them, I guess. I mean, the flowers in the front look very nice." Earl was desperately hoping he didn't sound too stupid. "Oh, and Pearl Sturner over at the Hy-Vee recommended this." He handed Marlene the box with the tart inside.

"Oh, my goodness," Marlene said, opening the box, "it looks delicious! All I had were some cookies! Thank you." She seemed to be genuinely pleased and this made Earl feel better.

He remembered the other piece of advice Nearly gave him— to make sure he listened. Women liked that, he said. Earl began to wonder how Nearly might know so much about women. They certainly both had relationships, but he was quite certain that women confused Nearly just as much as they confused him. This thread of thought was interrupted by Marlene's voice and the appearance of a slender young woman with short honey-colored hair—hair that seemed to stand on end as if she had just had an electric shock. The tips of each strand were the same blue as the hydrangeas in the front.

"Earl, this is my grandniece, Laurie. Laurie, this is my friend Earl Johansen. We've known each other since high school."

"Hey, Earl," Laurie said, shaking his hand firmly. "Nice to meet you."

Earl smiled and nodded, shaking her hand and having the first impression that Laurie seemed to be an attractive, friendly young lady. She was dressed mostly in black—black jeans, black T-shirt—the only thing not black was the decorative red stitching on her black cowboy boots.

"Laurie is visiting for the summer." Marlene's easy, friendly voice suddenly sounded as if she were making an effort at amiability. There was a pause.

"I'm here on probation, Earl," Laurie said with feigned embarrassment.

"Sorry?" Earl said.

"My grandmother is con-*cerned* about me so she thought a couple of weeks in I–o–way with Aunt Marlene might, like, do me good and y'know what?" Laurie's face opened up with a brilliant smile, "I'm havin' a *blast!*"

"Oh. Well … that's great," Earl said.

"Laurie, why don't you and Earl go on out to the porch and I'll put these flowers in some water and get the hors d'oeuvres."

"Right this way," Laurie said. "Isn't this a *great* house?"

"Yes, it's very nice," said Earl.

They walked into a three-season porch. It was so light and airy, Earl felt as though they were outdoors. He sat down on a small sofa. Laurie sat down on a wicker chair next to him.

"So …" Earl hesitated. Laurie's eyebrows shot up and she leaned in slightly.

"You're … enjoying your stay?"

"I really *am.*" She seemed to lean on words that Earl didn't expect to be emphasized.

"Where do you live?"

"Phoenix," Laurie said, leaning back in her chair and rolling her eyes. "Talk about the butt *end* of earth!" She leaned forward again. "When I turn eighteen, which is, like, not that far away? I am going to get out of that miserable town."

"Kinda hot there, I guess," Earl remarked. Other than the time he spent in Europe during the war, he never strayed far from Iowa. He had certainly heard that Arizona was hot. A dry heat is what people said. He wondered when Marlene might show up. "Lots of us older folks seem to like it in Arizona," he added, smiling.

"Yeah, that's true. But, like, *that's* not bad or anything, you know? It's just so conservative and gross. Too bad, too, because there are a lot of really beautiful places in the desert."

"Oh," Earl said, shaking his head as if he knew exactly what she was talking about. "I guess you need to live where you can be comfortable."

"Ex*a*ctly!" Laurie exclaimed. "I do *not* like the heat but, like, if I had to stay in Arizona? I would go to Tucson or someplace like that. Maybe Taos or someplace in New Mexico. Much better. More art and stuff. I think I might be a photographer. Like my dad."

"Oh, your dad's a photographer?" Earl said. He knew a man named Ralph Dvorak who used to take the class photos and graduation photos for the schools.

"Well," Laurie hesitated, "he didn't do it for a living but he really *could* have. He was good. I used to tag along with him on weekends."

Just as he noticed that she was talking about her father in the past tense, Marlene walked in. She carried a tray of several kinds of cheese and crackers that were not the Ritz or saltines he and Nearly had on occasion.

"What can I get everyone to drink?" Marlene asked. "I have red wine, beer, scotch ..."

"A beer sounds great," Earl said.

"Me too!" Laurie said with a grin. Marlene looked at her with eyes narrowed and then she smiled.

"Oh, all right. One beer."

"Aunt Marlene, you sit down. I'll get stuff. What do you want?"

"Red wine. Thanks."

"She seems like a nice kid," Earl said as Laurie left the room.

"Oh, she is. And very bright." Marlene looked off in the direction of Laurie's wake. "Very bright. But she and her grandmother—my sister, Muriel ... did you ever know Muriel?"

"I knew who she was but ... no ..."

"Well, Muriel and Laurie are ... Muriel's been taking care of her since her father died about a year and a half ago, and"— Marlene gave a half-smile—"let's just say it's been a little bumpy. Laurie was close to her dad."

"Where's her mother?" Earl asked.

"Rosemary—Laurie's mother. My niece." Marlene was looking at him but now her gaze left his face and dropped down to her hands. "Rosemary was not well. Mentally, I mean."

"Oh," Earl said. He was sorry he had asked because now Marlene seemed sad and distant. When she heard Laurie approaching, she suddenly perked up and said, "Laurie and I are having a wonderful time!" Earl was not the most perceptive deer in the herd but he sensed her forced cheerfulness. Thank goodness, Laurie seemed focused on balancing the tray with the drinks.

The three of them sat and chatted. Earl felt as close to comfortable as he ever did around people he didn't know well. And as he listened to Marlene and Laurie talk and laugh, he realized he didn't know that many people well. Just Nearly.

While they nibbled on the appetizers, Laurie talked about the new computer that Marlene had just purchased.

"It's still in the box." Marlene shook her head.

"No it isn't," Laurie said. "It is all set up and ready to go. *You* are going to love this! You'll be able to find stuff out without *ever* leaving your house!"

"Oh?" Earl said. He remembered hearing about UNIVAC in the 1950s. It took up an entire large room. Now here, four decades later, there were articles in the paper about computers that one could have at home. Earl didn't really understand what the big deal was or why someone would need one.

"OK, so ... like, when I go back to Arizona?" Laurie said, "Aunt Marlene and I can send messages back and forth to each other on the *computer*. Electronic letters!" Laurie began talking excitedly about the Internet, Web pages, chat rooms and a future she was obviously looking forward to. "I mean, oh my *God*! Someday, Earl, *someday* ... computers? They are going to fit in the palm of your hand! I am not kidding!"

"I can't even imagine," Earl responded, sincerely amazed.

"And the whole digital camera thing is mind-blowing," Laurie said. "It is going to be so simple! No more darkrooms, chemicals, *and*," she paused for dramatic effect, "a photographer will be able to see the photo right away, in their camera, and maybe even be able to crop it and everything before it's even printed."

He'd had a Polaroid camera once years ago that seemed space-aged. Earl felt the world moving in a blur around him.

Dinner was roasted chicken, small red potatoes, and green beans from Marlene's vegetable garden. Earl couldn't remember the last time he had had a meal that tasted this fresh and good. With the help of the beer and wine, the conversation continued to flow easily from this to that and back again.

"What do you hear from Mitchell?" Marlene asked. To Laurie, she said, "Mitchell is Earl's brother. He's a writer."

"Oh, I hear from him now and then. He sends a letter or a card and I write back to him. He's teaching up at the U of M."

"I thought his book was wonderful," Marlene said.

Earl nodded, not wanting to admit that he had not read his brother's book. He suddenly felt exposed. The book was, after all, based on Mitchell's life here in Campbell.

"So, Earl. Are you retired and stuff?" Laurie asked.

"Yes, I guess so. Sometimes I do some handyman things around town for people I know, but mostly I'm retired. I used to do repair and janitorial services at a couple of the banks in town. No one could ever accuse me of being ambitious!" he laughed. Marlene and Laurie were kind enough to laugh with him.

"What else do you do to stay busy?" Marlene asked. Earl had thought about this on his walk over to Marlene's. He had a hunch he would be asked what he does with his time.

"I do a little gardening. I have a small space near my house for vegetables. And," Earl said mostly to Laurie, "I visit Nearly. He's at the VA."

"Nearly?" Laurie said. "Is he another brother or something?"

Earl looked at her and smiled. "He's my friend. But I guess he's as close to a brother as anyone has ever been. I mean, Mitchell and I were never that close."

"And his name is Nearly?" Laurie leaned in, as if ready for a story.

"Yes. Nearly," Earl said, taking a sip out of his beer bottle. He decided he liked this young woman. She was different, sure, but as Marlene said, she was smart. "His mother never married but when she was pregnant with him she met an Irishman and they fell in love. They were going to get married but …"

"But what?" Laurie said when Earl paused.

"Sean Kelly died a week or two before the wedding."

"Nooo!" Laurie said. "Wow … how sad …"

"I had no idea," Marlene joined in.

"So, I guess his mother was in a bad way, heartbroken, you know. "Earl continued, "And because her son—if they had married—would have had the last name of Kelly, she took it as a last name anyway and named the baby Nearly."

"Nearly Kelly," Laurie said with a light laugh.

"I never knew this," Marlene said. "What a sad story."

"You know how it was, Marlene. It was hard for Nearly and his mom. She worked at the processing plant for the longest time." Earl looked at Laurie, realizing he had left out an important piece of the story. "Nearly's mom was an Indian from Minnesota. Ojibwe, I think. I was never sure how she ended up down here but I think Sean Kelly was from Ottumwa or something."

"Oh, wow …" Laurie said. "Well, that must have been awful."

"Nearly got picked on a lot. His mother sort of kept her head down, worked hard and tried not to be noticed."

They talked then about Nearly, his mother, how it was in mostly white, German or Scandinavian Campbell in the old days. They talked about the people who tried to be true Christians, treating their neighbors with love and kindness. They talked about the others who shrunk the Scriptures to fit in their own narrow, tiny world.

Marlene brought the tart to the table. "Now we're talkin'!" Laurie said excitedly and left the table to get the Reddi-wip out of the refrigerator.

"I think my dad knew Nearly's mom. Deborah, wasn't it?" Marlene said.

"Yes," Earl said. He remembered his own father making unkind remarks about Deborah Walking Elk Kelly and her "bastard" whenever they were driving past the small house where she and her son lived. He realized he wasn't sure what had happened to Nearly's mom. He knew if anything had happened to her, Nearly would have told him. A wave of sadness came over Earl. He felt as if he should have helped more, done more. Now he was getting old, and if Nearly lasted much longer it would be a miracle. Time was running away with everything.

Laurie returned to the quiet table. "God, how long was I gone? What's going on?"

Marlene smiled. "Nothing happened. Just thinking about Nearly."

What transpired next was not planned. It wasn't like Earl to share much. It took him a few seconds to realize that it was his own voice he was hearing. He told the two women about when he and Nearly came home from the war and Nearly wanted to speak over the public address system. When Earl and Marlene told Laurie about the loudspeaker, she began to laugh, almost choking on a mouthful of tart.

"You're kidding!" she exclaimed. "*That's* how they notified people?"

"That's how it was done for a long time." Marlene shrugged. "It's a small town." She and Laurie looked at Earl, who was gazing down at his hands.

"The thing is, I stopped Nearly. I didn't want him to make a fool out of himself or give anyone more reason to be mean to him. Or his mom. I stopped him, and he told me the other day … he told me it was his one big regret."

"Oh, Earl. I'm sure he didn't mean it …" Marlene began.

"I'm pretty sure he did."

A few moments of silence ensued. Laurie began peeling the label off a beer bottle. As she picked at it with her thumbnail she said, "Y'know, Earl, it's never too late to do stuff."

Earl woke early Monday morning to the sound of rain falling—a sound he loved and found comforting. Instead of getting up, he lay in bed listening as the drops landed on the leaves outside the window. He thought about the dinner at Marlene's. It was a pleasant evening—a ray of hope, even. He enjoyed meeting intelligent young people. He liked Laurie and guessed she would do well, whatever path she decided to take. When he began to ruminate over things he said or didn't say, he knew it was time to get up and start the day.

After breakfast, his plan was to go visit Nearly, but he thought he might wait until the rain let up a little. He sat at his sturdy kitchen table, pushed Mitchell's book to the side and looked through the *Des Moines Register*. The smoke from his cigarette streamed out the open window. There was a follow-up article about the woman who drowned her two kids. He shook his head to clear the image of two small children in a car, sinking. There was a review of the movie *Apollo 13*. He remembered when that happened, how it was all anyone could talk about, the astronauts stuck up in space. Earl wondered if someone like Laurie even knew that this event had occurred. If Nearly was well enough to go to a movie one of these days, maybe that was the one they would go see. Looking through his mail, he was pleased to find a postcard from Mitchell. The front of the card showed a rugged coastline and a caption "Greetings from Maine." Earl read the card: *Hi, Earl. Here in Bar Harbor, Maine, to give keynote speech at conference. Very pretty here but won't have much time to go sailing! Ha ha. Thinking of you—hope all is well. Mitchell.*

****

The rain let up just before 11:00. The humid air was swept away by a northern breeze that wafted the freshness of verdant greenery. The aroma from the processing plant would be in someone else's nostrils today.

Earl decided to walk to Della's Diner for lunch. He was two blocks away when he heard his name being called.

"Earl! *Hey*, Earl!" Laurie almost skipped across the street in her cowboy boots. She was still mostly in black, a tank top under a dark blue denim vest and some kind of black filmy skirt over black capri tights.

"Well, hi there," Earl said. He noticed that her backpack was gray.

"Where're you headed?" Laurie adjusted the backpack slung over her right shoulder.

"Oh, I'm going to Della's. Time for lunch."

"You want some company?" Laurie asked.

"Sure." *Now why did I say that?* Earl thought. He would be sitting and conversing with this young lady without Marlene's aid. Not only that, but he would be in a public place where many people knew him. What would they think?

"Cool!" Laurie said as they started walking. "I was just out taking some photos. The light around here is *incredible*! Especially after the rain. I got some shots of the sky. And the clouds. Wow!"

Della's Diner was in the middle of the block. To the left was a large, empty store that was once Munson's Furniture and Upholstery. For thirty years, Ralph Munson's family had owned the store. Ralph died four years ago and although his son, Richard, gave it a go, the kid's heart wasn't in it. On the right was Banks Dry Goods. Earl served with David Banks in the Army. He remembered David having a good head for figuring things out. Even though the phrase "dry goods" was hardly used anymore, David made it work. They sold Red Wing boots, good sturdy work clothes, Faribo blankets and other necessities. Things that people needed.

Della's was a long and narrow cafe. The twenty-five-foot-long counter, with the two-seat curve on either end, was on the left as Earl and Laurie entered. On the right a stretch of worn red vinyl booths. Della Marsh was a woman of indeterminate age. She and her husband, Andy, had owned and run this diner since 1948. *How old was she then?* Earl wondered. *Eighteen or nineteen?* One of the stories told in Campbell was that she had been there every day except for one week when she was in the hospital giving birth to their son, Henry, and two days when she was getting Andy settled into the Vets home. Looking at Della, he didn't doubt it.

"Well, Earl, as I live and breathe," Della said. "Who's this? This your granddaughter or somethin'?" Della's hair, once chestnut brown, was now steel gray, and done up in a bun.

Earl hesitated.

"Hi, I'm Laurie." The two women shook hands.

"Nice to meet you," Della said with a smile. "Well, go on and take a booth before they all get filled up. You want coffee?"

"Yes, please, I'll have coffee," Earl said.

"Do you have Diet Coke?" Laurie asked.

"Honey, I even have that cherry-flavored Diet Coke, although why anyone would drink it is beyond me," Della replied.

"Regular Diet Coke, please," Laurie said with a smile.

Earl noticed that Laurie did not correct Della's misconception that she was his granddaughter. Of course, neither did he. Thinking that Laurie (like many these days, he'd noticed) would not approve of smoking, they settled in a nonsmoking booth toward the front of the diner.

Placing her backpack gently into the corner of the booth, Laurie said, "So, what are you up to today, Earl?" Just then Della showed up with coffee and a Diet Coke. She took a straw out of her apron pocket and set it next to the sweating glass.

"Been out to the Vets lately?" Della said, resting the coffee pot on the table.

"I'll be headed over after lunch. How's Andy doing?" Earl replied. Della shook her head and frowned. "He's not so good. Sometimes he knows who I am and sometimes not. I went last night to see him and he called me 'Margaret.'" Della chuckled. "I spent the rest of the night trying to remember who in the hell we ever knew by the name of Margaret. Well, I guess it's partially my fault—I know he's worse in the evening. I'll send Sandy over for your order." Della started to walk away and then turned as if she'd forgotten something. "How's Nearly?"

"He has his good days and bad, I guess."

"That's life … it's always something," Della said and went back to work.

Laurie watched Della walk away, then took a long sip of soda through the straw as she looked at the menu. "What's good?"

"Well," Earl started, "Della knows how to make a mean burger. Her sandwiches are all pretty good too."

"Salads?" Laurie offhandedly asked.

"You know … I don't think I've ever had one of her salads." Earl confessed.

"Really? Not much of a salad guy, huh? What do you usually have?"

Earl did not have a "usual" here. Over the years, he had ordered almost every sandwich on the menu, plus quite a few of the dinners, or "entrees." In the thirty-plus years the diner had been open, there had only been about five or six menus. The last one changed the heading "dinners" to "entrees."

Ignoring her question and thinking she would, as young people often did, attribute it to an old man's hearing loss, Earl said, "I am going to have the BLT."

Earl's anxiety about not having Marlene there to guide the conversation turned out to be unnecessary. Laurie chatted about what she might do in the future ("maybe photographic design using computers"), places she would like to see—Paris, London and New Zealand—and about missing her dad.

"It was really, really awful, you know? Cancer is just a *bitch*. I felt so bad for him and there wasn't anything I could do. I felt so …" Her eyes filled with tears. "He was a good guy."

Earl was a little uncomfortable. Here he was, sitting across from a young woman who was on the verge of weeping. Laurie wiped her eyes on her sleeve and said, "I'll bet *your* dad was great,"

He looked at her, unsure of what to say.

"My dad?" he said. "No, my dad was not a great guy. Just the opposite."

"Really? Like, what? He was mean or something?"

Her innocence was touching. She had grown up with a father who loved her and, most likely, a mother who loved her as well, although from what Marlene started to tell him last night, he wasn't sure about Laurie's mother. He was fairly certain that no one beat her or ridiculed her friends. Earl tried to imagine how that must feel.

"Yes, he was mean."

"That must have sucked," she said.

"It did," Earl replied. "It sucked." He looked into his coffee cup as if a message was there on the bottom—as if he were drinking tea and hoped the leaves would tell him what to say next. "But," he added, smiling, "my grandmother was a strong woman. She was something."

****

Hiding in the large closet, the sound of dishes shattering on the floor made her flinch. Breathe, she told herself. Just breathe. One of two things would happen: he would find her and later pass out or, if she could stay hidden, he might pass out before he discovered her and forced himself on her again. Deep breath, that's it. Dear God, why? Why?

She found herself thinking about her meeting with Pastor Anderson. As she reflected on what the pastor had told her, she began to feel something shift inside. "Verna, it is terrible, what drink does to a man," the pastor said. "This is Arne's cross, this weakness. You made vows to one another and to God, so I know this will pass. Help him, Verna. Be his helpmate. Walk with him through this desert, as the apostles did with our Lord."

As the apostles did with our Lord? she thought. First of all, Jesus was by himself in the desert. Secondly, as soon as the going got tough, those men skedaddled. They couldn't get far enough away from Jesus! The women were the ones waiting on our Lord's body after that horrible crucifixion! But John stuck around too, she remembered.

She named her first child John after that loyal disciple. And now Johnny was buried in the cemetery next to her mother and father. Her daughter, Anna, was spending the night at a friend's house. That was providence.

In the darkness of the closet, she did her best to blend into the corner, hiding behind the two long winter coats that smelled of stale alcohol and nicotine.

"VERNA!! GET OUT HERE!" Arne shouted drunkenly. He was coming into the room. "Bitch …" he mumbled. "A man has rights … fucking bitch …"

The closet had two doors. If he opened them both, the light would pour in and he would surely see her. The left door swung open but— Verna would later take this as one of the greatest blessings of her life—the right door was stuck. "Son of a bitch …" Arne pulled on the door, "goddamn door. SON OF A BIIIIIIITCH!" Arne kicked at the door, screaming. There was a groan and a thud. Then silence.

It took a moment for Verna to realize she'd had her eyes shut tight. She opened them, and tried to peek out from behind the coats. Through the one open door she could see him lying on the floor.

Verna quietly stepped out of the closet, taking care to walk over his legs.

"Uhnnnhhh …" he groaned. The sound made her jump.

She looked at him. How could God want her to stay married to this sorry excuse of a human being? Marrying Arne was a mistake, one she figured out too late. He was charming right up to their *wedding night. Then it was like that book,* The Strange Case of Dr. Jekyll and Mr. Hyde.

"Uhh ... god ... help ..." *Arne slurred.* "I think ... my heart ..."

He's having a heart attack, Verna thought. She went into the kitchen.

"Verna, don't leave ... baby, please ... help me ..."

Her good dishes lay on the kitchen floor in shards, a bizarre unfinished mosaic. The carving knife was on the counter. She grabbed it just in case Arne was faking.

Anger bloomed with each step she took back to the bedroom. If she had to use the knife, she would. Self-defense. She had endured enough. If this was the life God wanted for her then let God live with Arne. Somehow, she would make ends meet. Getting Anna away from this nightmare, getting both of them away from it was all that mattered.

"Verna ..." *Arne moaned, clutching his chest.* "Jesus ... my chest ... help me ..."

"I'm going to help you, Arne," *Verna said. Her voice was steady but her hands shook as she set down the knife on the night table. She picked up the pillow from her side of the bed, placing it gently under her husband's head. A while back, Verna recalled, Arne thought the pillow was too soft.*

"Call somebody ... call the ..."

Their phone was not working, having been ripped from the wall during his last tirade a few nights ago. Their neighbors, Betty and Jim, had a working phone. "Don't worry. I'll go to Betty and Jim's and call," *Verna said. She picked up the other pillow from his side of the bed. His first pillow wasn't hard enough. It set him off. He twisted her arm behind her, almost breaking it until she promised to replace it with a harder pillow. This one.*

It wasn't easy. He was a big man. But he was a big, drunken man whose heart was punishing him. He flailed. Kneeling and steadying herself on one arm, she only had to fend off one grasping hand as she pressed the pillow over his face. A woman gets strong working in the garden, hauling wet clothes to the clothesline, lifting children.

It was cold outside. A scent of approaching snow filled the air. She had taken a moment to put a new pillowcase on Arne's hard pillow, and placed it back on the bed. The old pillowcase went into the hamper. She closed Arne's horrified eyes and shut his wide-open mouth. Leaving the broken dishes where they were, and returning the knife to the counter, she set out for her neighbor's house.

****

Earl picked up the tab for lunch. He felt it was a nice thing to do for someone visiting Campbell. He was ready to go outside, light up and stroll over to see Nearly.

"Hey, Earl?" Laurie said. He looked at her. "I was wondering if you could look at a couple of photos my dad took and see if you know where these places are."

"I haven't traveled much, but let me have a look," Earl said, taking his reading glasses out of his shirt pocket.

"No ... no, they're here, in Campbell or at least some place around here," she replied. "Aunt Marlene said she wasn't sure but that you might know."

Laurie removed five photographs from a cardboard envelope. The pictures were black-and-white, each one vivid and slightly haunting, the mind searching to fill in color and nuance.

Earl looked at the photographs one by one. The first was a shot of dark swirls of clouds above a cornfield still lit by the soon-to-be covered sun. Another was a barn, obviously in disrepair, worn wood, a rusty tractor. "That looks like the Sjordal place. I think someone bought it and fixed it up." The next photograph made Earl stop. It was a small, well-built house, and sitting on the front step, an Indian woman displaying a small quilt. "Well, I'll be ..." he said.

"What?" Laurie said.

"Remember I was talking about my friend, Nearly?"

Laurie nodded, taking a last sip of her Diet Coke.

"That's his mother," Earl declared with a slight smile.

"What?" Laurie leaned forward, looking at the photograph upside down. "Really?"

"That's his mom. I'm sure of it. When did your dad take this photo?" Earl asked. Her dad couldn't have been that old when he died. Laurie was, what? Seventeen? It was hard to tell how old Deborah was in the photo.

"I don't know. There wasn't any date on the back and I haven't gone through his negatives."

"Well, if you ever do, I sure would like to know."

Laurie and Earl stood outside the diner.

"Thanks for lunch!" Laurie said cheerfully.

"It was nice talking to you," Earl said. "I certainly enjoyed the photos. I hope I'll see you again." And he meant it.

"Me too."

Earl started to walk, taking out the pack of cigarettes and shaking one loose, when suddenly Laurie ran back to him and said, "Would it be OK if I came to meet Nearly sometime? Maybe show him the photo?"

"I'll ask him," he said. "I'll ask him."

****

"Thought you might not come," Nearly said as Earl walked into the room. Nearly was propped up but slightly slouched in his bed, the small quilt like a cape around his shoulders. On his nightstand, a well-worn book open, looking like a tent, its spine pointed toward the ceiling. *Huckleberry Finn*.

"I'm here," Earl said. "It was raining pretty good so I thought I'd wait." Earl pulled up a wooden chair that reminded him of the solid oak seats in grade school. He looked around the room. The other bed—Carl's bed—lay there, the mattress stripped of its clothing. A movable curtain divided the room in half when there were two residents living there. It was open all the way to the wall now, indicating that Nearly—at least for a little while—had the room to himself.

"So?" Nearly said.

"Where's Carl?" Earl asked.

"Carl?" Nearly echoed. "I think he got moved or died or something."

Earl looked at his friend. "When did this happen?"

"Yeah. I don't know. Maybe yesterday?" This came out sounding as if Nearly was in school, guessing at a question directed at him by the teacher. A few seconds passed and his face brightened. "You gonna tell me about your date? I've been wondering," Nearly said, folding his hands on his belly.

"It wasn't …" Earl stopped. He took a breath. "It was a very nice evening. I met Marlene's grandniece, Laurie. Very nice young woman. She lives in Phoenix and is just here for a few weeks, visiting Marlene."

"Surrounded by women." Nearly said. "I don't know if I'd know what to say. Did you bring flowers?"

"I did," said Earl. "And when I was at the Hy-Vee, guess who I ran into."

Earl didn't mean for it to be a real puzzle, but Nearly seemed to be considering it with care.

"I guess I don't know," he said at last.

"Pearl Sturner."

A chuckle moved Nearly's chest and shoulders. He coughed and chuckled some more. "You didn't tell her where you were going, did you?"

"I did."

"Oh, *jeez*," Nearly was coughing and laughing.

"I know, I know." Earl smiled. "You're thinking she went and told everyone I was seeing Marlene."

"I don't *think* she did. I *know* she did!" Nearly said. Earl had not seen Nearly this animated in quite some time.

Earl decided to detour the train of conversation. He told

Nearly about the dinner, what they ate and a little of what they talked about.

"This young lady knows about computers and all sorts of things. Very bright."

"She live here?" Nearly asked.

"No, she lives in Phoenix. She's just visiting," Earl repeated.

"Phoenix," Nearly said. "I met this guy, he was a Navajo. Met him, oh … let me think … it was at one of those shows we went to during the war."

"A USO show?" Earl asked. He wasn't at all sure where Nearly was going with this. There were many days when Nearly's thoughts rambled, and Earl had to repeat things. The rambling and repetition didn't irritate him, though. The thought that one day he wouldn't hear the stories or have anyone ask him the same thing over and over, however, did bother him.

"USO!" Nearly said with as much enthusiasm as he could muster. "I saw Betty Grable and Bob Hope. What a show!"

He stopped talking and picked at some lint on the sheet.

"You were saying about the guy you met. The Navajo? Phoenix?" Earl prompted.

"Oh," Nearly said. "Yeah, he was a Navajo. All of us Indians used to find each other at these things. He was in this unit and I can't remember what they were doing but anyway he told me I should come to Arizona. I told him I was fine in Iowa."

It sounded to Earl that the story had just ended.

"I don't remember if you ever went there," Earl said.

"Nope," Nearly replied. "Just fine right here."

After a respectful pause Earl said, "The young lady I met …"

"Lindy," Nearly said.

"Laurie," Earl corrected.

"Laurie," Nearly repeated.

"She showed me some photographs her dad took. I guess he used to live around here or at least he lived in Iowa."

"What was his name?" Nearly asked.

"I don't know," Earl said, suddenly embarrassed that he did

not know the man's name. "But anyway," he continued, "she has this photograph and, Nearly?"

"Yup."

"I am pretty sure it's a picture of your mom. And she's holding up that quilt."

"What quilt?"

"That one there—the one around your shoulders."

Nearly lifted his right arm, reaching stiffly behind him, his hand grazing his ear. He tugged on the quilt and had a look on his face as if he was relieved to find it there.

"There it is," he said. "There's a picture?"

"I'm pretty sure it's your mom."

"You should show it to her," Nearly said.

Earl rubbed the side of his face.

"What's the matter?" Nearly said, concerned. "Oh. Did she pass?" His face was suddenly shadowed in sadness.

"No, no," Earl said quickly. "I just keep forgetting she's still here because I so rarely see her. Tough little bird. You're seventy-two or something like that, right? I mean, how old was she when she had you?"

Nearly pursed his lips and looked up thoughtfully. "I think she was seventeen or eighteen. Maybe nineteen."

"So she's, what? Close to ninety I'd think," Earl asked.

"I guess. She writes me letters sometimes and sometimes she'll call. Not often. She was never much of a talker." Nearly leaned his head toward Earl. "She stops by but not very often. I think she's afraid to come here because she thinks they might not let her out!" He laughed and started coughing again.

Earl met Nearly's mother only a few times—once at their high school graduation, another time just after the war. About fifteen years ago, when Nearly was thrown in jail for driving without a license, he saw her again. Lars Petersen, whose brothers had taunted Nearly through high school, was the arresting officer. Earl contacted a man he served with in the Army. The guy was now a lawyer in Iowa City. This is what Army buddies were for, he thought. When they stepped outside the courthouse, Nearly's mom was waiting. Deborah Kelly was a small woman of bone and muscle and uttered few words. She faced the lawyer and said, "My son did not belong in jail."

"No ma'am," the lawyer said, "You are correct. We don't jail people for driving without a license. We give them a ticket."

She continued to look at the lawyer. He looked back at her.

"Your son was jailed for driving while being an Indian."

Earl looked at his friend. "Well, the next time you hear from your mom, say hi from me, OK?"

"Sure. I always tell her about you. She's real happy that you come to visit me."

Earl looked down at his shoes, cleared the small lump in his throat and looked up again. "I was wondering if you would like to meet Laurie and maybe see the photo."

"OK," Nearly said pleasantly.

"Good. I'll find out when she might be able to come."

Time passed, the minutes filled with talk and pauses. Earl could see that Nearly was getting tired. As he stood to leave, Nearly said, "Hey, Earl? Be sure to tell me when that girl is coming to visit, OK? I'd like to look nice."

The midsummer clouds formed a soft web between the sun and the earth. It was hazy and warm, the time of year when the earliest hint of fall was not far off. The local advertising circular that arrived every Tuesday contained a page with local news. Lenny Gustafson's grandson, Alex, was going to the Minnesota State Fair in August to show his pigs. They won blue ribbons at the county fair a week ago. Lenny's daughter, Ellen, her husband, John, and their three children lived just across the Iowa border in Canton, Minnesota. Earl was sure that Lenny was proud of his grandson. Every now and then, especially when he met a young person who was personable and smart—like Laurie—Earl had a twinge of wondering if he had missed something by not having children and grandchildren. His mind would then wander to *what if he had a child and didn't know it?* It was remotely possible.

It wasn't difficult to find a time for a visit. Earl was retired and Laurie was on vacation. Marlene decided to drive them to the Vets Home, where she would stop and say hello to Nearly, then go off to her bridge game—this week at a friend's house in Jordan Springs.

As they walked in the front door and started down the hall, Earl nodded at Wilma who was standing at the nursing station. Seeing him with two women caused her to relax a little. She smiled and returned the nod.

His familiarity with the building made him feel as though he were leading a tour through a museum no one wanted to visit. The place wasn't perfect, but it was better than having these guys out on the street with nothing and no one.

"Just a second," Earl said as they approached Nearly's room. "I'll check and see if he's ..." Earl stopped. The room was empty. The beds were bare. He felt his heart deflating, falling to his stomach. "Oh, God, no," he said hoarsely. This moment waited in the hallways for him every time he came here to visit Nearly. There wasn't another person in the world Earl was closer to, not one other soul he trusted as much as he trusted Nearly. They had saved each other.

****

An apple orchard spread for several acres on the edge of Campbell. A farmer by the name of William McKinley Hutchinson owned it and the adjacent farm. Everyone in town knew him as Old Hutch. As children, Earl and Mitchell could escape to the orchard when the air at home became stale and thick. Their father was easy to anger, and both boys learned early on to read the signs and get out of the way.

Earl sat down underneath one of the trees, deep in the orchard.

He didn't know what to do. He couldn't go home. Not yet. He had to think. How was he going to face going to school tomorrow? If word got out about what he did, he'd be in deep trouble.

He thought about his options. He could be sick. Looking up into one of the trees, Earl thought about jumping from one of the higher branches and maybe breaking an arm or a leg. For sure he wouldn't have to go to school, plus it would distract his family. But it was Friday tomorrow and if he was sick or if he had a broken leg—no baseball game after school and stuck in the house all weekend. He'd have to find a way to avoid his father. Running away was always a plan. But how far could a kid get without any money? Nobody had any money these days, he thought.

Over the past couple of years what Earl heard from adults were conversations about people who once had more money than they could spend in a lifetime and how these rich folks lost it all. Tales of wealthy people shooting themselves or jumping out of the windows of the tall buildings that they had built spread around the town like a virus.

The citizens of Campbell seemed to bond in hard times, and these were the hardest they'd seen. Last March, a town meeting had been called. The mayor made his announcement over the loudspeaker system: *CITIZENS OF CAMPBELL. THERE WILL BE A MEETING SUNDAY AFTERNOON AT 2:00 AT FIRST METHODIST. PLEASE COME IF YOU ARE ABLE. THERE WILL BE REFRESHMENTS.*

The refreshments were slight but appreciated. It was a sure-fire way to get people who were running out of resources to come to the meeting. Earl and Mitchell went with their mother. It felt safer than staying home. Their grandmother, Verna, sat in the front row.

The mayor started the meeting by thanking everyone for coming. Jack Thompson was forty-two years old. That night, he looked about ten years older, tired and pale.

"I love this town," he started. "You all know that. Most of you knew my folks." He paused. "And I think we can help each other through this mess. Now, we don't know if these programs the new president is talkin' about will work …"

One of the farmers sitting in the back of the church said, "It'll work! Has to!"

Earl's grandmother piped up and said, "Oh, sit down, Albert. We all know you voted for FDR." A ripple of chuckles broke up some of the heavy air.

"I don't care much if you all think I'm some kind of a socialist or something," Jack said. "I just want us to … maybe have … just throw some ideas out there. Let's help each other through this."

There was a stillness in the room. People looked at their hands, at their shoes. After thirty seconds that felt like an hour, a deep baritone voice spoke.

"Well, this has been on my mind." It was Old Hutch. "Farms have been hit hard these days. We all know how good the land is. I believe there's nothing an Iowa farmer can't grow."

"'Cept for bananas!" someone joked. Again, the low laughter seemed to lift the air.

"OK. Bananas," Old Hutch conceded, smiling and rubbing the stubble on his chin. "I'm just sayin' maybe a cooperative of some kind. Sharing seeds, farm equipment and such. We kind of do this informally anyway, on a neighbor basis, so it might work."

The conversation went from there and long into the night. More meetings followed. There were a few people who had a what's-mine-is-mine attitude, but most could see that sharing seeds and produce and helping one another was a whole lot better than eating dust. A community co-op was one idea. A potluck dinner every Sunday evening was another. Everyone was encouraged to put their scraps of food—when there were any— into one of the four composting bins in back of the Methodist church.

****

Earl sat in the orchard, thinking. Why didn't he just stay out of it? He just made his life a whole lot harder, that's for sure. He was going to be in deep trouble whether he showed his face at school or at home. But what else could he have done? Walked away? Earl sat on the ground, his back against a tree, his hands holding an empty paper sack, his mind going over the events of the afternoon.

He left school that day and stopped at the co-op for a cup of sugar. "One cup, Earl," his mother said, "no less, no more. Whatever you do, don't spill it. If your dad doesn't get a cake for his birthday … well …" She grimly shook her head.

As he left the store with the precious sugar in a small sack, he rounded the corner and saw two boys from school, the Petersen twins. Their father was the town barber. The twins, Nels and Anders, were thirteen but looked as though they were seventeen. Tall, blond and broad-shouldered, they stood a full foot taller than their younger brother, Lars, who was in Earl's grade. The Petersen boys had some kid trapped against the wall. At first, Earl thought they were harassing their little brother, but as he stood watching, he knew it wasn't Lars. This kid had black hair. There were only two people in town with black hair—Deborah Kelly and her son, Nearly.

"Hold him, Anders!" Nels barked at his brother. Anders stood at Nearly's back with the poor kid's arms pinned behind him. Nels had something metallic in his hand. Just as Earl was going to turn around and avoid the whole mess, he saw Nearly look at him, his dark eyes open wide, glistening. Earl's throat felt like he had swallowed sandpaper. He heard his grandmother's voice in his head: "You remember that I am always proud of you, you understand? The only thing you need to do is always try your best and do what you know is right."

He heard Nels say to his frightened victim, "Gonna take some of your hair, chief. Isn't that what you Indians do? Scalp the white folks? Huh?" Nels and Anders were laughing. One of them said something about "a bald Indian."

"Hey!" Earl shouted, the sack gripped in his right hand.

The two blond heads popped up. He could see their blue eyes from where he stood.

"Get outta here, Johansen," Nels said, lowering the arm and hand that held what Earl could now see were a pair of scissors.

"Unless you wanna get messed up," Anders added.

Damn, these guys were big, Earl thought. "Just knock it off. Let him go." His voice came out loud but shaky.

"Oh, so you're an Indian-lover, huh?"

Earl stood there. He could feel sweat trickling down his back and into his underwear. "C'mon, you guys. Let him go."

This brief exchange must have distracted them enough to allow Nearly to tamp his panic down and think. In the space of ten seconds, in one fluid motion, Nearly's foot stomped on Anders' instep and continued a trajectory of knee to Nels' crotch.

"RUN!!" Nearly screamed. "RUN!!"

Earl hesitated for three seconds and then took off. Not knowing where to go, he followed the blur that was Nearly, moving as fast as Earl had ever seen anyone go. Nearly was headed for the orchard where he quickly climbed up into a tree. Earl climbed into the next tree. He thought the sound of his heart beating could be heard for miles and would most certainly give them away. The Petersen boys were big and strong but their size made them slow. And Nels couldn't be feeling too good right about now. The only thing distracting Earl from his current predicament was the limp, empty sack in his hand. He must have snagged it on a branch. There was a glittering trail of sugar on the lower branches.

He looked over into the next tree. Nearly was absolutely still. He glanced over at Earl and put his finger up to his lips.

When they thought the coast was clear, the boys climbed down from their respective trees.

"Thanks," Nearly said, watching grains of sugar sparkling,

fluttering out of the hole in the depleted sack. Some of them clung to Earl's pants.

"It's OK," Earl said.

"You kinda saved me," Nearly said.

"Nah," Earl replied, adding nervously, "You don't think they'll come back, do you?"

"Might. Anyway, thank you."

Earl nodded and then looked at the sack and felt a rock in his stomach. Sugar was a luxury. How many times had his mother and grandmother told him that? And for his father's cake. He may as well go home, take his dad's belt and start beating himself with it. Earl looked up to say something but Nearly was gone.

There he sat, no closer to a solution to his problems. Earl wondered how much time had passed—twenty minutes, perhaps thirty? He heard someone coming. He had seen rabbits when they were terrified become absolutely still, eyes wide, body on full alert. That was him right now. Maybe it was the Petersen twins. Maybe they would beat the ever-lovin' crap out of him and put him out of his misery. His whole body exhaled as he saw Nearly approach.

"Hey," Nearly said.

"You scared me," Earl said, brushing off his pants as he stood. "I thought it was Nels and Anders."

"I can't stay. I just came back to give you this." Nearly handed him a small paper bag. "Thanks again."

Earl looked inside the bag.

Sugar.

****

"What is it?" Marlene asked, looking into the room. "Oh!"

Several thoughts ran through his head as he began to measure his loss. He didn't get mad too often, but he could feel the heat rising inside, his muscles tensing. *Why didn't they call me? I'm on Nearly's list. They're supposed to call me if anything happens.*

"Mr. Johansen!" It was Wilma. She was practically running. "Mr. Johansen!"

There was a hint of anger in his voice as Earl took two steps toward Wilma. "Why wasn't I called?"

"Called? Why would we call you?"

"I'm on his list. If anything happens to him, you're supposed to call." Earl knew he was repeating himself. He couldn't think.

"Nothing happened to him," Wilma said. "We just moved him to another room."

Earl stood there staring at Wilma. He suddenly remembered Marlene and Laurie. They were standing to one side of the door.

"Oh! Oh, well … look, I'm … I'm sorry. I thought …"

"Yes, I know," Wilma said. "I think Mr. Kelly is sitting in the day room but for future reference, he's been moved to room 124." She patted his arm, turned and walked briskly down the hall.

Earl felt dizzy. He held on to the metal railing that ran along the hallway, took a deep breath and released it.

"Are you all right?" Marlene asked with deep concern.

"Yes. I'm OK. I just … for a minute there …" Earl stammered.

"*That* was scary," Laurie said.

For some reason, Laurie, with her musical young voice chiming in like that made Earl smile. "It was," he said. "I'm OK now, though."

Sitting in his wheelchair, wearing worn charcoal-gray corduroys and a white shirt, Nearly looked refreshed. And for a moment, Earl almost forgot how sick his friend was. Nearly's hair was clean and he wore a black bolo tie with an agate pendant. Earl was so happy to see him he wouldn't have cared if he'd been dressed in a ratty and stained old bathrobe.

"Hi," Earl said cheerfully. "I brought visitors."

When the introductions were made, Nearly said, "I got a new room."

"Wilma told me. I went to your old room and it was empty.

Scared the dickens out of me. I thought maybe we'd lost you," Earl said. His tone was meant to be lighthearted, hoping to cover how shaken he still felt.

"Nope. Not yet. Still here. Hey, guess who I ran into," Nearly said and without waiting for a reply, continued, "Lars Petersen."

"What?" Earl said, startled. "Here?"

"Yup. He's an inmate. Been here a while. I just keep forgetting to tell you."

The word "inmate" made Laurie laugh.

"Actually, I didn't run into him. He ran into me. Hit me with his wheelchair."

Marlene engaged Nearly in conversation and Laurie joined in, talking about their visit, what they had done so far, and what their plans were.

Earl wasn't happy to hear that Lars was anywhere around. His brothers were role models in how to be mean. And now he was at the VA.

"So, did you know that Marlene here went out with this guy?" Nearly said, jerking his thumb toward Earl and smiling.

"No! No *way!*" Laurie said, looking at her great-aunt.

"Oh, for cryin' out loud," Earl said.

"We went out—twice, I think," Marlene said quickly. "Perfect gentleman."

Earl's face felt hot.

"So what did you guys do on your dates?" Laurie asked.

"Well," Earl started. "Nobody had any money so sometimes we just got together with other couples, went to the creamery for ice cream. Movies weren't that expensive, maybe twenty-five cents."

"And they showed two movies, not just one." Nearly added helpfully. "Plus a newsreel. Sometimes a cartoon."

Laurie looked at Marlene and said in a teasing tone, "So, you *dated*, huh?"

Earl was sensing that either the conversation or being here in God's waiting room made Marlene uneasy. This was confirmed when she suddenly stood up, and took Nearly's hand. "I'm sorry, I have to go. This has been fun. Nearly, it was so good to see you."

"Good to see you too, Marlene. Be sure to keep an eye on Earl."

Marlene hesitated a moment, still holding Nearly's hand. "I … I will."

"Your game isn't until when?" Laurie said.

"I'll see you later, OK?" Marlene hurriedly said to Laurie. "Dinner might be a little bit later, maybe 6:30."

"I'll walk you out." Earl offered. He got up from his chair, preparing to escort Marlene to her car.

"Oh, thanks, Earl, but I think I can find my way. You enjoy your visit. We'll talk soon."

That whole business with Nearly's empty room made her uncomfortable, he thought. He wished he had handled it better. As he watched her leave, he saw a man in a wheelchair sitting in the corner, watching.

Lars.

Earl took a look at him and then returned to his chair. From the quick glance, Earl could see that life had run over Lars a few times and was now dragging him along. The face was still hard. The eyes were still the same cold blue as they'd always been.

"Earl tells me you take photographs," Nearly was saying to Laurie.

"Yeah!" Laurie brightened. "This is so *cool*. My dad lived around here and he used to go out and take photographs. I'm trying to find the places in some of his photos and then take them again. Like an updated shot, y'know?"

"What was your dad's name?" Nearly asked.

"His name?" Laurie paused a moment. "Ben."

Nearly considered this information, nodding his head a few times. "That's a good name. Ben."

"Show him the picture your dad took …" Earl began.

"Oh, yeah! This is so … I don't know … it's just like … strange.

But in a good way," Laurie said, pulling out the cardboard sleeve that held the photographs. She handed the photo to Nearly.

After looking at the photo for a moment, Nearly smiled and said quietly, "That's our house. And that's my mom. I have that quilt."

"Really? *That* quilt?" Laurie was surprised.

"How old was your mom then?" Earl asked, thinking that might give them an approximate year when the picture was taken.

Nearly looked closer at the photograph, lost in moments he spent sitting on the porch, talking with his mother. "She worked on it when I was overseas in the Army. She called it her safety quilt because she was sure if she kept working on it, I'd be safe. Plus, she sewed some birchbark inside of it. Little pieces." He was memorizing the photograph.

"Why did she do that?" Laurie asked.

"For protection." He looked up at Laurie. "I guess it worked 'cause here I am! Of course, she didn't give me the quilt until I got sick and ended up here."

Laurie reached into her backpack and pulled out her camera. "Do you mind if I take a picture of you?"

"I dunno. Might break your camera," Nearly replied shyly. Suddenly he said, "Take one of me and Earl."

There were possibly only three or four photos that existed of the two men together. Earl had one in a frame at home. It was taken the last night before they went to basic training. On the back written in Nearly's scrawl: "Civilians no more!"

As Laurie took some candid shots, she kept her subjects engaged with questions and conversation, keeping them distracted from the fact that they were having their picture taken. Earl wondered if she learned that from her dad.

"Were you guys together during the war?" she asked.

"No, we were in different units," Earl said. "We wrote to each other." He didn't expect to have his picture taken today. *Sure hope I don't look as off-balance as I feel*, he thought.

"Funny thing is, we were at Normandy together but we didn't know it until after," Nearly said.

"What? How did that happen?" Laurie said, the mechanical butterfly wings of the camera shutter softly and swiftly opening, closing, opening, closing.

"It was a pretty confusing time," Earl said. "Turns out we were both on Utah."

****

Nearly was trying to remember what it felt like to be bored. Up until about a week ago, his time in the Army felt like long stretches of learning how to assemble and disassemble his firearm, broken up by physical labor, card games and writing letters. He would enjoy being bored right now. Bored, warm and dry.

The landing was a blur of smoke, acrid air and deafening noise. There were seventeen men in his squad when they hit the water. They had lost two so far. Now, lying in a hole meant for two men, he found it barely long enough to stretch his legs out, and he wasn't a tall man. Nearly did his best to figure out what was going right. At the moment, he was not being shot at and the noise had stopped. That was enough. He knew it would all start up again. They were moving toward some French town, or at least that's where they were supposed to be heading. It wasn't his business to ask any questions about why, but he really did wonder about the how after he overheard a conversation between Captain Burrows and Lieutenant Morelli.

"What *is* this shit? Bushes?" Burrows said.

"Sir, according to Sergeant Rousseau, they're hedgerows."

"Hedgerows. Nice. I guess our intelligence wasn't too intelligent," the captain drawled. "Well, what the hell. Let's figure out how we're gonna do this, Lieutenant."

A sudden explosion rained dirt onto Nearly. A soldier dropped in next to him. It was a tight fit.

"Sweet Jesus!" the man said. The man looked at Nearly. "Private Dan Sweet," he said, holding out his hand.

"Private Kelly," Nearly replied. The two men shook hands. Private Sweet's eyes were two blue lights shining out from a young face covered with dirt and grime. A lock of damp hair the color of corn silk poked out from underneath his helmet.

Another explosion. Others around them opened fire. They did the same, raising themselves up enough to shoot through the thick growth at whatever or whoever was on the other side and then tumbling back down into the hole. This was repeated— isolated shots, some artillery fire, some mortars—and then silence.

Before darkness surrounded them and the Germans started their nighttime bombing raids, Private Sweet and Nearly dug their hole a little longer and deeper and set up a shelter half.

"Where are you from?" Private Sweet asked while they worked.

"I live in Iowa," Nearly said. "Small town."

"I'm from Tuscaloosa, Alabama. Big town." Sweet grinned. "I wanted to have an adventure. I'm not so sure about it now."

"Me too," said Nearly. "Sounded like a good idea at the time."

Progress was measured not in miles, but by how many fields were crossed. The hedgerows made it almost impossible to know who might be on the other side. Nearly wondered about Earl. The last letter made it sound like he might be part of this mess too, but he couldn't be sure. Other than wondering about Earl or his mother from time to time, Nearly didn't think about home too much. Best not to.

When dawn came, the men were gathered together.

"Our resident artist, Corporal Kaufmann," Burrows began, "has volunteered to risk his ass to make sure we might be able to figure out where we are and what might be in front of us. He is going to draw a bee-yoo-tee-ful," he looked directly at Kaufmann and smiled, "and accurate map." Captain Burrows looked at the young faces that had aged considerably in the space of a week. "We need a few volunteers to go with Kaufmann. I'll give y'all a minute to contemplate whether or not you'd like to be a part of the fun."

Nearly reached into his small front pack and took out a metal tin that was not GI. He walked over to the corporal.

"I just wanted to say good luck and thought you might want to have a couple of smokes," Nearly said.

"Sure, thanks. Mine are mostly busted," Kaufmann answered. "Where did you get the tin?"

"Oh, I've got a bunch of 'em. They used to have mints in them but the cigs fit real nice in there. They don't break and they don't get wet." Nearly handed the metal container to Kaufmann and then added, "You're an artist?"

"Well," Kaufmann replied, "I guess I can draw. I like to draw cartoons, mostly."

The captain walked up to where Nearly was standing with Kaufmann.

"Private."

"Sir," Nearly responded.

"Good of you to volunteer. Who else?" Burrows looked around, then called out "Private! Both of you." Burrows pointed at Sweet and another man, Private Sloan.

Volunteer? Nearly thought. *Oh, holy shit.*

Lieutenant Morelli led their small reconnaissance party. Nearly wasn't that fond of Morelli. From the very beginning, the lieutenant called him "Chief," and there wasn't a damned thing Nearly could do about it.

They walked hunched over; they crawled. They stopped to allow Kaufmann time to quickly sketch and then continued on a path that, back in more bucolic days, was a peaceful way to get cows and sheep to various fields and pastures. At one point, while Kaufmann was sketching, Nearly and the two other privates lay on their bellies and did their best to peer through the hedgerow.

"Like a freakin' fence. Only natural-like," whispered Private Sloan with a heavy Brooklyn accent. "Should have these at home."

The three men took their knives and cut away at the thick hedgerow. Nearly made a hole and then wished he hadn't. Directly on the other side, approximately fifty feet away, were a dozen German soldiers headed right toward them.

Sweet and Sloan looked through the hole, their eyes wide, and the three privates scurried back to where Kaufmann was finishing his sketch. The lieutenant sat next to him, alert.

"Sir, a dozen German … the enemy … they're right on the other side of that …" Nearly almost got out the whole sentence before the shots started. A path sat down from the hedgerow. There was an embankment about two feet high that provided some protection. Morelli got up on his knees and started firing. The other four men followed their leader, popping up, firing, then ducking down against the safety of the embankment. Nearly had no idea if he was hitting anyone, he just kept returning fire. Private Sloan took out his grenade and looked at the lieutenant, who nodded. Standing, Sloan wound back like a center fielder throwing to home plate and pitched the grenade over the hedgerow. The grenade blew.

And then he fell.

Nearly turned to get Sweet to help him grab Sloan's body. Sweet's once bright blue eyes were dull and staring. Blood from the huge hole in his throat covered the front of his jacket. With his hands shaking, Nearly reached into a pocket and took out a piece of birchbark tearing it into two small pieces. He tucked them into the pockets of the dead warriors.

"Chief!" Morelli called hoarsely. "Get over here! Kaufmann's shot."

"Sloan and …"

"I know, I know. Just …" Morelli suddenly stopped as if he heard something. Nearly heard it too. Silence. They stared at one another for five seconds.

Kaufmann had been hit in the shoulder. Morelli and Nearly did their best to stop the bleeding. "I'm OK …" Kaufmann said with pain in his voice. When they had the wound packed as well as they could, they helped him to his feet.

Morelli picked up Sloan's body in a fireman's carry. Nearly did the same with Sweet. They were sweating under the weight of the bodies, stopping only once to rest, catch their breath, and take a sip of water from their canteens. The three men said nothing to one another, alert to every sound. With a nod from Morelli, Nearly hoisted Sweet across his shoulders, relieved they weren't that far away from where Burrows and the rest of the men waited.

After debriefing with the captain, Nearly collapsed into his shelter hole. He tried to sleep but could not get Sweet's dead face out of his mind. He started a letter to Earl.

Dear Earl, I don't know where you are right now—sure wish I could talk to you. I'm still alive and that's more than I can say for a lot of guys …

"Oh … Kelly?" It was the lieutenant. Nearly stood and felt the ache in his back from carrying his dead comrade.

"Yes, sir?"

"Kaufmann wants to see you."

Nearly fell in a couple of steps behind Morelli. When they were five feet away from the medic tent, Morelli suddenly stopped and faced him.

"Kelly," Morelli began, "I know you've taken some shit from some other guys, about being an Indian and all." Morelli had been looking down at his boots. "I heard it. Didn't do anything." He then lifted his dark eyes and looked directly into Nearly's face. "I just want you to know that you did good today. You're a credit to the unit and … and you're a good guy." He turned to leave, took a couple of steps and called over his shoulder, "Anyone gives you trouble? I'll take care of 'em."

****

Private Kaufmann was sitting on a cot, his left arm in a sling, a small ditty bag next to him. "Hi!" he said as Nearly came into the tent.

"How's the shoulder?" Nearly asked, taking a seat on an empty cot across from Kaufmann. He had never felt so tired.

"It'll be OK. I guess I'm headed for an LST and then to a hospital ship or something," Kaufmann said.

"Well, that's good—you get to go home, huh?" Nearly said.

"I don't know about that, but …" Kaufmann let the sentence fade. "I never thought I'd be much of a soldier anyway. Not really my thing but I wanted to do my bit." He shrugged his good shoulder. There was a pause as Nearly simply nodded his head.

"I wanted to show you something." Kaufmann reached into the ditty bag with his right hand. He pulled out a small metal tin. Nearly recognized it as the metal box he had given to Kaufmann, the cigarettes. Except now it had a ragged tear in it. Kaufmann held it up. "This thing here?" he said. "If it wasn't for a bunch of paper and this tin, I'd be a goner." He handed it to Nearly and continued. "Instead of a big hole in my heart, all I have is a bruise."

Nearly examined the box. There were small shreds of tobacco and the hole made by either a bullet or a piece of shrapnel. The tear was larger on one side and quite a bit smaller on the other.

"I had all my paper, the map I was working on folded up too. Wish I could've saved it just the way I took it out. Big chunk of metal. Morelli took a picture of it, though. I'll send it to you when I get home."

"That would be something to see," Nearly said, handing back the tin to Kaufmann, who took it and said, "I just wanted to say thanks."

****

Laurie and Earl walked together out of the Veterans Home.

Earl found himself wondering about Marlene and if she was OK. She left in such a hurry. He had been thinking about her more often since their dinner.

When they reached the edge of the VA property, Earl said, "Well, Laurie, it was nice seeing you again. Hope those pictures come out."

Laurie nodded. "I think they'll be great," she said. She didn't make a move to leave, just stood there as if her body was waiting for her mind to give the command. "I'm going to help Marlene do some canning tomorrow. New experience for me!" she suddenly said.

"Oh," Earl said, surprised. He wasn't sure where this was leading. "Like what? I mean, what kinds of things are you canning?"

"She has a bunch of stuff in her garden that she puts away for the winter," Laurie said. "Y'know, stuff like beets and green beans. I guess she has a bunch of tomatoes. Stuff like that." It was said as if she were telling him about the dirty laundry she had to wash, a task that was less than appealing to her.

"My grandmother used to do that. Canning," Earl said, trying to lend something to the conversation.

"Yeah, well ..." Laurie started, "I guess I'll learn how tomorrow."

"Well, I hope you have fun," Earl said, touching the brim of his cap and taking a couple of steps.

"Hey, Earl?" Laurie said. "I'm gonna be here for, like, another week, week and a half or so. I was wondering if you might want to have lunch again."

Earl didn't know what to make of this. Why would this bright, young woman want to hang out with a worn-out old man? Of course, what else did she have to do here? Campbell wasn't exactly a hub of activity for young folks.

"That would be nice," he said.

"How about day after tomorrow?" Laurie posed.

"All right," Earl replied. "Della's. 11:30."

He lit a cigarette and thought about Laurie's invitation. He wasn't sure why she wanted to have lunch again but he figured he had to eat anyway. He walked to the Hy-Vee before heading home. His thoughts returned to the visit with Nearly. Looking back on it, Marlene seemed quite concerned when Earl had that heart-stopping moment of thinking Nearly had died. She didn't seem uncomfortable until that whole business of their dating came up. *I suppose she didn't want to talk about things like that in front of her grandniece*, he thought. His internal critics, the ones with his father's voice, started in. *Maybe she was embarrassed. It's not like I was ever a great catch or anything.* About a block from the Hy-Vee, Earl stopped walking. He crushed the cigarette butt under his shoe. *Shut up,* he said. *Just shut up. I had a very nice time with Marlene and Laurie the other night. Just shut up.* He knew he had not heard the last of that dark chorus.

He thought briefly about how unsettling it was to see Lars Petersen at the VA and hoped there wouldn't be trouble. He thought about Nearly and how good he looked today. The guy really made an effort. This made Earl smile. In the not-so-distant future was a room with his own name on it, that much was certain. Maybe a room at the VA, maybe somewhere else, but it was there. Waiting. Who would he have to get dressed up for?

At the grocery store, Earl decided he would get a pork chop or something, maybe some green beans or some other kind of vegetable. An argument could be made for eating better, not eating so many frozen dinners, which were full of salt and other stuff that couldn't be good for him. Since he walked everywhere, he was sure he got his exercise, and that was good. But he did smoke. That was a problem. Of course, when it came right down to it, there weren't many great years ahead so why should he care about what he eats? Pretty much too late now. He found it difficult to think about actually cooking a meal for himself. Besides, it was easier to go to Della's or to the bar for a burger.

****

His dreams that night were all jumbled images: Marlene, a plate of pork chops on a hospital bed, Lars Petersen racing in his wheelchair, and Nearly holding up a gold handbell, ringing it.

It was the phone that woke him up. Earl looked at the clock. 11:45.

"Yes …" he said, and then tried to clear his voice.

He walked along the faded yellow hallway of the hospital wing. The air was a dank, rich mix of human smells, ammonia, rubbing alcohol and uneaten food. Earl approached the nurses' station. His mouth was dry.

"Nearly Kelly?" he asked.

The young nurse wore light blue cotton scrubs. Earl wondered how old she was. As he got older, it was harder to tell a young person's age. They all looked to be teenagers.

"He's in 410. It's just down the hall here," she said, pointing.

Nearly lay in the hospital bed. An oxygen mask covered his mouth and nose. Wires came out from under a faded gown that was once white. It had what looked like little gray-blue stars all over it. The wires were connected to a machine that showed his heart rate and blood pressure. It beeped softly. Nearly's arms lay at his sides. Earl pulled up a chair and touched his friend's arm.

"Hey, Nearly, it's me," he said. "Earl." he added, just in case.

Nearly's eyes fluttered a little. He was saying something but the mask made the words hard to understand.

"Citiiiiizz … kkohhhhllll …."

Earl leaned closer. "What? I can't understand you." He thought he saw a smile form under the mask.

"Citiiiiizz uff Cuuummmbblll …" the garbled sounds came out again. "Isss isss Meeeeleee …"

Earl was going to lift the mask but his intention was interrupted by the arrival of a nurse wearing dark blue scrubs.

"Hi. I'm Hanna." She walked over, took a look at Nearly and at the numbers displayed on the machine. "He's looking better already!" she chirped.

"Can you tell me what happened?"

"Are you his brother?" she asked.

Earl weighed the urge to lie and found it too light. "I'm his friend," he said, adding quickly, "I'm on his emergency call list."

"Oh. OK. Well, it looks like it was a bit of congestive heart failure combined with an insulin reaction. But we'll get him back to normal."

This woman was too happy for Earl's liking. Not that normal for Nearly was any picnic, but how do you get a person back to normal if his heart has failed?

The nurse left the room. Nearly kept muttering. Earl lifted one side of the oxygen mask. The words came out slurred but crystal clear to Earl. Nearly was making his announcement. "Citizens of Campbell …" he said.

Earl sat next to Nearly's bed, dozing off and then, when his head lolled to the side, waking suddenly. Not knowing how much time had passed, his eyes popped open when he heard a familiar voice say, weakly, "Hey!"

Nearly had his head turned toward Earl. The oxygen mask was hanging beneath his chin like a clear plastic goatee.

"Hey," Earl said, shifting forward in the chair and rubbing his neck. "How're you feeling?"

"Oh, I dunno. Must've passed out or something. I guess I feel better. Kinda hungry."

Earl was relieved to hear him talking, glad to hear he was hungry. That was a good sign. After an hour or so of sporadic talking and watching Nearly charm a couple of nurses, Earl started his walk home, feeling tired but much better than when he'd arrived.

Returning home from the VA, Earl was so exhausted that he fell asleep on top of his bed still wearing his clothes. When he finally woke up, it was almost 9:15 the next morning. Sun poured through his window. Earl couldn't remember the last time he slept past 7:00. He could feel the synapses in his brain trying to move through fuzz.

Starting the coffee was the first step. While it was brewing he took a shower, scraped the gray, bristly whiskers from his face and prepared to go back to the hospital to check on Nearly's progress.

Sitting down, he looked at the basket he kept on the kitchen table. He put his mail in the basket and then, once a week, sorted through it. Seems the only things in there were bills, ads and requests for money. The reward for donating even a small amount to an organization was a never-ending request for more money and more return address labels than he would ever use. He thought he might take a minute to sort through the small jumble of envelopes after he had something to eat.

Halfway through his bowl of raisin bran, the phone rang. It was Janet Carlson from down the street.

"Hi Earl. I'm sorry to bother you," she began. Like Earl, Janet had lived in Campbell since Doc Schmidt delivered her at her parents' home. She had a daughter named Pauline who grew up with the nickname "Pinkie." Pauline Carlson left Campbell to go to college and ended up at Harvard, eventually becoming a lawyer. One would think this would be a source of pride but all Janet ever did was natter snide comments like "I think she got a little too big for her britches at that hoity-toity school."

Janet was calling about her sink. "Well, now Janet," Earl began, "I'm going to tell you the same thing this time I did the last—you need to replace that faucet."

"How about if you pick out a faucet for me and I'll just pay you to do that and make it all right?" she said. "$75.00?" she proposed. "I'll let you use my car." The mail sorting would have to wait. And he supposed Nearly was doing well enough that his visit could be postponed for a couple of hours. That is how Earl found himself at Janet Carlson's kitchen sink, Janet dangling the keys and smiling.

Earl had only driven a car once since he shut the door of his garage on his Chevy Caprice. His neighbor Willis needed to go to the emergency room after driving a large nail through his right foot. Earl drove Willis's Oldsmobile, a big tank of a car. Driving it made him nervous and tense, just like he felt now driving Janet's Honda Civic. As soon as he stepped foot into Campbell Ace Hardware, he was breathing easier. He knew there would be more choices of faucets at the Menard's out by the freeway, but that would have taken more time and he wanted to get this done. Walking on the wood floor back to the plumbing department, surrounded by everything a person might need to build or repair things, Earl felt himself relax. This store gave him comfort.

By the time he had finished the job, walked home and got cleaned up, it was close to 1:00 and Earl was hungry. He ate a peanut butter sandwich while standing over his sink. Janet had offered him lunch but he declined. Late last fall, he was there repairing the faucet and as he was sitting on the floor to look under her sink, she placed her hands on his shoulders and massaged them while he tried to work. What Earl gleaned from other guys who were handymen, electricians and carpenters, was that Janet had an awful lot of things that didn't work in her house. Lunch was not always lunch, and he did not want to give her the wrong idea.

As he was going to open the door and start his walk to the VA, his phone rang. Three seconds seemed to tick: *Don't ... answer ... it ...* but he did. It was Marlene. After some pleasantries, she asked, "Have you seen Laurie?" Marlene sounded tense.

"No. Why? Is she missing?" Earl asked.

Marlene told him that Muriel had called, just wanting to check in and chat with her granddaughter. At the end of the conversation, Laurie was in tears and ran out of the house, not wanting to answer any questions.

"She's fine, I'm sure," Marlene said trying to convince herself. "It's just that I'm responsible for her and I'd like to know where she is."

"She's probably out taking pictures or something." Earl tried to sound reassuring. "Tell you what. When I'm done visiting Nearly, I'll give you a call and see if she's shown up. If she hasn't, I'll help you look for her."

****

The light came through the window at the end of the hall on the fourth floor of the hospital. Even backlit, Earl could see the shape of Nearly in a wheelchair. He was talking to someone. Earl thought it might be a nurse or an aide who had taken a liking to Nearly. It wasn't uncommon. When people took the time to speak with him, they always ended up liking him. As Earl approached, he saw that the person Nearly was talking with was Laurie.

"You're looking better," Earl said to his friend as a greeting.

"I think I am." Nearly smiled weakly. "Still feel a little tired, though."

"I see someone got your quilt for you."

The old quilt was lying across Nearly's lap. He patted it softly and said, "One of the nurses."

"Laurie," Earl said, nodding at her. "This is a surprise. Thought you'd be up to your elbows canning tomatoes!" He tried to make his greeting light, as if he didn't know anything about what had happened. Laurie gave a quick shrug of her shoulders.

"I had a little … I was …"

"She had a difference of opinion with her gran-momma," Nearly said helpfully. "I was just sayin' to her, that kind of stuff happens all the time. Especially when you're young." Nearly's voice had lost some of its strength, not enough air to lift it.

"Sorry to hear that," Earl said to Laurie. *Poor kid*, he thought.

Relationships were a bit like opening a stubborn jar lid, not knowing exactly what might be inside. That's what Earl thought. You work and struggle to get the dang thing open and when you finally do, there's joy and relief. But what's inside? You never know. Sweetness, perhaps. But sometimes a complicated mix of vinegar, dill, garlic and small cucumbers. Still good, but not sweet. And maybe not what suits your taste at the time. But there you are with the jar open, never to be sealed again.

Earl could not fathom what the relationship must be between grandmothers, mothers and daughters. Women. He was pretty sure that women were smarter than men. Even though his mother and grandmother didn't see eye to eye on most occasions, they had a kind of emotional shorthand.

A while back, while he was waiting at the dentist's office, he picked up one of the last beat-up magazines on the table and reluctantly—and somewhat uncomfortably—skimmed an article about estrogen. On top of making women unpredictable, he was sure estrogen must give women that bond, that secret language they have.

Now, the relationship between fathers and sons? It was a minefield. Earl believed that a father ought to teach a son how to be responsible and take care of things, something his own father never did. He learned how to be a man from his grandmother. Maybe it didn't have anything to do with being a man, he thought. Verna taught him how to be a decent person.

Laurie sighed heavily, bringing Earl back from his thoughts.

"It wasn't that big of a deal, I guess," she said. "I wanted to stay here with Aunt Marlene."

"You mean you wanted to hang around Campbell a while longer?" Earl said with mock amazement. "Gosh, I don't think I've ever heard anyone want that!" he chuckled, and nudged Nearly with his elbow, hoping he was cheering her up.

"I *like* it here!" Laurie said emphatically, looking at Earl, her lower lip trembling. She looked down at her lap. "I can't talk to my gramma anymore. She just doesn't get me. My dad did," she said. "I'd rather stay here." In a very soft voice she added, "People are nice here."

"Bet she'd miss you though," Nearly said, glancing over at Earl. Earl nodded in agreement, squeezing the edges of his Cubs cap as he looked at the logo.

"There's not much to do here, Laurie," Earl said kindly. "I mean, I know you like being away from home and your aunt is such a nice person …"

"It's never gonna happen." Laurie cut him off. "My gramma said she might let me—*let* me," she added with emphasis, "stay here another week. It's not like she's my mother or anything."

Nearly nodded, his face a portrait of concentration. He had taken a shine to Laurie. Earl could see that from the first visit.

As the two of them chatted comfortably, a memory took hold of Earl. He remembered a rare scrape from his youth. It was when he was a junior in high school. He overheard Lars Petersen compare Nearly to a puppy.

"Kelly? Kelly'll go anywhere with anyone if they're nice to him," Lars snickered. His friends laughed. The words acted like a match to a short fuse inside Earl, who was walking by at that moment. Earl turned around, grabbed Lars by the shirt and slammed him up against the bulletin board on the wall.

"Shut up!" Earl shouted into Lars' shocked face. "He's ten times the person you are, you little creep."

It was Earl's bad luck that the principal, Mr. Preston, and another teacher were starting down the hall at that precise time. Since Earl was clearly the aggressor, the two men told him to apologize.

"Sorry," mumbled Earl. "Shouldn't've gone off like that."

"I'm surprised, Mr. Johansen. Now shake hands with Mr. Petersen and let's not have any more of this," Mr. Preston commanded.

After school, Earl went to help his grandmother with some chores. The dust-up at school had turned him sullen and silent.

"I hear there was some trouble at school," Verna said. Earl was shoveling some compost onto the garden and working it into the soil. He didn't feel like talking. *How in the heck does she know about this?*

"Earl, look at me please," Verna said. Earl sighed heavily and stopped what he was doing. He turned to face his grandmother.

"Boys get into scrapes all the time," she said. "What was this about?" Earl reluctantly told her about what had happened, the unkind comment. Verna noticed her grandson had grown tall over the summer. Either that or she was shrinking. She had to reach up to put her hands on his shoulders. She looked at him and said, "Try your best to not push people around, Earl—I know sometimes it's hard, especially for boys. Girls push people around in a different way, I guess." She squeezed his shoulders affectionately. "Don't go down the road to being a bully. The world doesn't need any more bullies. We've got plenty. And those Petersen boys …" Her voice trailed off as she turned to put a few more late tomatoes in her large apron pocket. Her back to her grandson, she added, "I'm glad Nearly has such a good friend."

"Come back and see me," Nearly said to Laurie. "Bring some more pictures." Laurie promised she would return, but told Nearly she was not sure about bringing photos.

"Depends on how they turn out," she said.

"I don't know a good one from a bad one," Nearly said. "I just know the ones I like." He then admitted he was ready for a nap.

"Next time you come, I'll be back in my room," Nearly said. "It's a different room."

"I know," Earl said, pushing the wheelchair down the hall.

Leaving the hospital, Laurie asked Earl if they were still on for lunch the following day.

"Well, sure," he responded. "If you still want to."

"OK," said Laurie. "Della's at 11:30?"

Earl noticed a slight hint of a smile on her face, the first time that day she seemed to lighten.

"Della's, 11:30," he confirmed.

"Hey, would you do me a favor?" Laurie asked.

Earl felt himself tense even as he nodded. This one request— *would you do me a favor*—was often loaded with unforeseen trouble. There was usually more to the question, and once the question was asked, he could hear the rest of it in his head: *because I just can't face it (or her or him)*.

"Would you call Aunt Marlene and tell her I'm OK? I'm gonna go for a walk on my way back and maybe take some shots. I don't want her to worry."

"Sure," he said.

Laurie wandered by the Sjordal farm. She found the place where her father must have stood, taking the photograph of the run-down barn and rusted tractor. Earl was right. Someone had fixed the place up. No longer looking as if it might collapse under its own weight, the barn stood with straight, plumb walls. It was painted deep red with white trim. On top, an iconic rooster weathervane shuddered with the light, warm breeze. In her father's photo, the fence had boards missing, posts leaning. The fence Laurie now looked at was sturdy, straight and white. The rusted tractor was gone. Reaching into her backpack, she took out her small tripod, her camera and the old photograph. Alternately looking into the viewfinder and then at the photograph, she tried to frame it exactly.

After her father died, her grandmother started going through his things too soon for Laurie's liking. Perhaps it was grief—she had already lost a daughter —but it felt like she was in a rush to get rid of any trace of Ben Carver. Laurie was confused and angry. Why would she just trash his stuff?

She had come home from school to see boxes and bags sitting out by the trash cans. Horrified, she grabbed the flat boxes she knew held her dad's photographs and negatives and ran into the house.

"What are you doing?" she cried.

"Laurie," her grandmother started. But the young girl's rage was boiling over. The sound of blood rushing around in her ears made it impossible to hear her grandmother.

"How could you do this?" Laurie spat. "These are *his* photos, *his* work."

"His hobby," Muriel said. "I didn't throw away *all* of them," she said defensively. "I kept the photos I wanted, of you, your mother, our family. But there are so many. I don't have anywhere …"

"I want them. I want *him*." Laurie cut her grandmother off. Tears ran down her face. "I want him. If you throw one more photograph away, I am out of here. I will never speak to you again. Never."

After retrieving the rest of the boxes, she went to her room and closed the door. She stayed there, refusing her grandmother's peace offerings of dinner and then later, dessert. Laurie sat at her desk. One by one, each photograph was scanned with the loving eyes of the photographer's daughter. In total, there were six large, flat boxes, all of them crammed with images her father had captured. Out of the boxes containing photographs of the family, her grandmother had taken the ones she found meaningful. There were multiples of each pose: Laurie and her mother at the beach, first day of school, family picnics, first bicycle; a picture of Laurie at twelve years old taking a picture of her father taking a picture of her. In another box there were stunning images of the desert in Arizona and Utah, shots of Big Sur, Yosemite, along with ribbons and certificates of achievement from art fairs and juried competitions.

One box was full of images of Iowa.

And now she was here herself. She played with shutter speed. After each soft click and whir, she'd look up, half expecting to see the farm as it was when her dad recorded his impressions. In these places where she knew her father had stood and fixed his artist's eye on the landscape, she felt close to him again.

When she was satisfied with her work, Laurie carefully stashed her equipment in her backpack and wandered down the dirt road.

She liked it here. Why couldn't she stay? Every time she thought about going back to Phoenix and having to endure another year at Pullman High School, Laurie felt as though she were draped in hopelessness. Her grandmother and her Aunt Carol were always trying to get her to join in doing girl stuff, like shopping or going out to gabby lunches. She never failed to make a disparaging comment on what Laurie wore.

"Are we going Goth?" her grandmother would smirk. *So stupid*, thought Laurie. *Just because I'm wearing black? She doesn't even know what Goth is! Like I'd ever go Goth.*

For Laurie, it was the time with her dad learning about the camera that made her feel like she was connected to him, continuing his art of interpreting a world that was rotating and spinning faster each day. She treasured their time in the darkroom, his teaching her how to develop photographs by the eerie glow of the safelight. In winter of her sophomore year, her life changed. She used to love the Christmas season. Now it was a reminder of what she had lost. All that was left of her father were a few cameras, boxes of pictures and a bright, strong thread Laurie felt running through the fabric of her life. She was only five when her mother died and mostly remembered her from the pictures her dad had taken. Her father's death had changed Laurie, turned her gaze inward. Even her closest friends were telling her to lighten up, that she was being a drag. Laurie tried but found no comfort in their conversations about boys, movies or who was doing what with whom. It was as if she sat by a puddle while her heart longed for the ocean.

Walking, lost in her thoughts, she suddenly realized she was at a dead end on top of a small hill. It was time to turn back. She owed her great-aunt an apology for running out the way she did.

As she was about to leave, Laurie noticed a worn path that made its way down to a small house that sat off another county road.

"No way," Laurie said slowly under her breath. She crouched on the ground and took out the photograph of Nearly's mother sitting on the porch of her house holding the quilt. "No way," she repeated softly.

Laurie's focus on the photograph and the small house was so intense, she didn't hear anyone approaching. An old voice soft as calf leather startled her, making her jump to her feet and turn.

"Can I help you?" the voice said.

Laurie's whole body felt charged. She found herself facing a very small, old woman leaning on an intricately carved cane. The woman wore a large beige sun hat and a denim shirt under a cloth vest. Beaded on the vest were bright red flowers, leaves in combinations of green, white and blue on multicolored stems and tendrils. The woman's jeans were worn supple from walking, bending, kneeling. Her skin reminded Laurie of a walnut shell, brown and deeply lined.

"I … I'm …" Laurie stammered. "Sorry. I wasn't …"

"Nice day," the woman said, looking out over the hill. Laurie nodded in agreement, looking at the woman and trying to wrap her head around the reality that this woman had to be ninety years old.

"Are you Mrs. Kelly?" Laurie blurted.

"I'm Deborah Kelly. Yes," she replied quietly, looking at Laurie. Laurie felt like every fiber of her soul was exposed.

"I'm Laurie Carver. I know your son. Well, I don't know him, exactly, but I've met him and I …" The words were spilling out too fast and Laurie could hear voices in her head telling her to be quiet. Deborah Kelly waited.

Laurie took a deep breath and started again.

"Well, see … my dad used to live around here and he took pictures. And he took one of you." She was still holding the photograph. She handed it to Deborah Kelly, who took it without moving her eyes from Laurie. Then, the old woman peered at the picture, and Laurie could see Nearly's face there, looking at it intently.

"That's a while back," she said softly. "Gave my son that quilt."

"I know. I saw it. I mean, he has it," Laurie said.

Deborah Kelly continued to look at the photograph and then handed it back to Laurie and looked at her. The calm of this woman was a little unnerving and it made Laurie want to fill up the spaces.

"I have my dad's photos that he took around here and I'm trying to take them again. Y'know, a then-and-now kind of a thing," Laurie explained. "Would you mind if I took your picture, like, you sitting on the porch of your house?"

After a moment, Deborah Kelly looked at her home and, with noticeable stiffness, started down the path. Laurie felt sure this singular opportunity had been blown. Then she heard the quiet voice say: "I might even have a quilt. You can tell me how my son is doing."

****

Marlene's wasn't too far out of Earl's way. It was a pleasant day and it felt good to be outside after spending so much time in the hospital. As he was about to knock on Marlene's door, it opened.

"Earl," she said, "Did you find Laurie?" Marlene's face betrayed her worried heart. He was glad he had good news.

"Well, I did," he said. "Wouldn't you know, she was at the hospital visiting Nearly."

"Thank goodness … the hospital? What happened?"

He realized then that he had told her he was going to visit Nearly. He didn't tell her anything about the phone call or what had happened.

"Oh, he's OK. He had some kind of heart trouble and diabetes trouble and ended up in the hospital. This isn't the first time. Probably won't be the last," Earl said, trying to sound nonchalant. "But he'll be back in his room by tomorrow."

Visibly relieved, Marlene said, "Would you like to come in? I just made some iced tea. I have soda too. Or I could make some coffee."

"Iced tea sounds just fine," Earl said, stepping through the doorway.

They sat out on the porch, just as they had that evening when Earl first met Laurie. Why did it seem like such a long time ago?

"I'm so glad you found her. I was worried…" Marlene said, setting the sweating glasses on coasters.

"I probably should have called or had Laurie call right away but she and Nearly were talking." Earl paused. "She seemed pretty upset."

Marlene sighed and took a sip of her iced tea.

"I'm just glad she's all right," she said. "Things will work out. They most always do."

After a brief pause Earl said, "She sure seems to have been close to her dad." He was curious about Ben Carver but hoped he wasn't being nosy.

"Very," Marlene replied.

"She showed me some of his pictures."

Marlene brightened. "Aren't they something? He was a talented guy. And a nice man."

"So, you said he died last year? Must've been pretty young."

"He was almost sixty." Marlene noticed the brief puzzled look on Earl's face. "He was quite a bit older than Rosemary. In his forties by the time Laurie came along."

They sat in silence for ten or fifteen seconds. Earl liked Marlene. She was smart, easy to talk to, and quite attractive. It had been so long since he had asked a woman out on a date he wasn't sure how to go about it. He frowned.

"Is something wrong?" Marlene asked.

"No!" Earl replied quickly. "No, just … thinking that it's hard to be a young person these days." It wasn't really a lie. He honestly did believe what he was saying. It was not, however, what he had been thinking.

Marlene smiled and nodded. "I think it's difficult to be young. Period."

****

The Laurie that showed up at Della's at 11:30 the next day was not the Laurie that had been sitting next to Nearly in the hospital. She seemed very much the way she was when Earl first met her, as if the sun were a helium balloon hovering above her shoulder, tied to her with an invisible string.

As she slid into the booth, she greeted Earl.

"You are *not* going to believe what happened to me!" she said, beaming.

"My goodness!" Earl said. "I guess you'd better tell me." He was smiling back at her. He couldn't help it.

Laurie unfolded the story for him—her walk, how she missed her dad and how close she felt to him as she stood taking the updated photo of the Sjordal farm.

"And then I just sort of started walking and I guess I wasn't paying much attention to where I was going," she said. "I was feeling bad about being disrespectful to Aunt Marlene and *then* …" she paused. *And then what?* Earl thought. She was a good storyteller. He felt as though he had been reading a book and suddenly the pages were missing.

"The road ended. But not really."

After placing their order, Laurie told Earl about meeting Deborah Kelly, about taking a photograph of Nearly's mother holding a quilt on her porch, just as her father had done all those years ago.

"I hardly know what to say," Earl responded.

"It was …" Laurie paused, shaking her head slightly. "It was like being with a really wise person. She's got this kind of … I don't know … a mysterious vibe—but not in a dark way."

Dipping the corner of his grilled cheese sandwich into a puddle of ketchup, Earl took a bite. Laurie had also ordered the grilled cheese along with some fries. Between bites, Laurie filled him in on the other places she had been in and around

Campbell, duplicating her father's old pictures and taking new ones of her own.

"Y'know, the more I see my own work," she said seriously, "the more I am convinced that maybe I am *supposed* to be taking photographs. Like it's fate or something." She chewed thoughtfully on her sandwich. "I mean, if you don't follow your dream or at least try ..." her voice trailed off.

"Well, yes, if you have a real drive or have a talent for something," Earl said, adding, "I never did." Laurie looked at him.

"There's nothing you ever really wanted to do?" she asked.

"Nothing that requires talent," he laughed.

"There must be something, Earl," Laurie said, trying to encourage him.

But there wasn't. He was content to walk around Campbell, do odd handyman jobs for people, visit Nearly, shoot some pool, go to the movies. If there was a gene for ambition, he didn't have it. Perhaps this was enough: to be a good neighbor, a good friend, a kind presence in his little spec of the universe.

"Not really," he replied.

"How about travel?" Laurie asked. "Everyone likes to travel." Earl looked at her, thinking that she was young and her life was full of possibilities. Laurie's world was expansive. His world was gradually shrinking. "Anywhere you want to go?" she asked.

"I guess I've always thought maybe going back to France and seeing where we landed during the invasion might be interesting."

The only other person he had mentioned this to was Nearly, whose reply was, "I'm not going back there. I'm OK staying right here." Returning home, Earl's sense was that—for some vets—sitting on the front porch until they knew for sure they were safe, hoping that what they saw and what they did might fade, was the only dream they owned.

But Earl wanted to see the landing site at peace. About a dozen years ago, he decided that he might go anyway. He had almost saved enough money and then life happened: root canal, crown, a new furnace. Last summer, he thought about this trip again as the country celebrated the fiftieth anniversary of the landings, but he shrugged it off. It was too late. And he was getting too old. Instead, he bought a large book of pictures taken by several *Life* magazine photographers, showing the black-and-white images of the D-Day landings next to color photographs of what these beaches look like all these years later.

"Sounds like a great trip! You should go!" Laurie said excitedly. Earl shook his head.

"No, I don't think so. Travel is expensive and besides, I don't have anyone to go with."

"But they have these group things!" Laurie exclaimed. "They even have ones for … for … older people. Seniors."

Earl knew the only thing he could say to stop this line of conversation. He smiled and said, "I guess I'll have to think about it."

"Are you blowing me off?" Laurie said, smiling.

"A little."

After a silence that was much too short for Earl, Laurie said, "It's just that I think people need to do stuff that they want to do." Laurie looked at Earl and then ate her remaining fries.

"What are you going to do today?" Earl asked, attempting to move the conversation away from dreams and what he did not do.

"More picture taking. Aunt Marlene and I might go to the movies tonight. How about you?"

Earl thought going to the movies with Marlene sounded like a good way to spend an evening. He suddenly remembered a line from a poem, something about the road not taken. Robert Frost, he thought. Frost or Sandburg or one of those guys.

"Earl?" Laurie said. "Hello?"

"Oh. Sorry. I was just thinking." Before she could ask what he was thinking, he said, "Well, I'll go see Nearly, I guess, and then I need to tend to some repairs around the house." Earl smiled.

"Maybe I'll come with you to see Nearly. Would that be OK? I wouldn't stay long," Laurie said. "If it isn't, that's OK. I can go another time. I wouldn't want to, y'know, intrude or anything."

Before Earl could respond, Della came by to deliver their check.

"How was everything today?" she said.

"Great!" Laurie said. "The fries are so good."

"Everything was just fine, Della." Earl said.

Laurie excused herself and headed to the restroom. Della set the coffee pot on the table. "Say, have you heard anything about the meeting the other night. The council?"

"No," Earl said. He did his best to keep up on what was going on in Campbell but did not go as far as attending council meetings. "Why?"

Della shook her head. "I was hoping you knew something. Ed Hinz was in here having a fit about some plans to tear down the old town hall buildings and replace them. You know how Ed is about historic buildings."

Earl knew that Della meant the town hall itself, the library and the old public works building that housed the defunct public address system.

Earl agreed with Ed. These were fine, sturdy brick buildings.

"They're going to tear them down?" Earl asked incredulously.

"That's what I heard."

"I guess I'll ask around," Earl said. "But I would imagine you'll hear more about it than I will."

Della nodded. "You have yourself a good day, Earl. Say hey to Nearly if you see him."

As they walked to the Veterans Home, Earl was lost in thought. Why in the world would the council want to tear down perfectly good buildings? These structures have withstood tornadoes, windstorms, torrential rain and burning sun. Now they're not good enough? He suddenly became aware of Laurie's voice: "Of course my grandmother doesn't think so. But I figure she only has me for another year. Eighteen is the magic number."

"Eighteen?" Earl tried to catch up. "Eighteen what?"

"Eighteen years," Laurie said. "Then I'm an adult. I can do what I want."

Earl smiled, wondering if she realized that responsibilities soon outweighed the freedoms of being an adult. But here she was, with her hopeful vision of the near future, and it was not his place to spoil it.

Nearly never looked what would pass for well, but today, instead of tired, he looked as though even speaking taxed what little energy he had. Earl noticed something else: he seemed worried. Anxiety was a common feeling for many people, but in all the years of their friendship, Nearly was rarely bothered with worry.

Seeing that Nearly wasn't in the best condition for visitors, Laurie left after about fifteen minutes, saying she was going to take some pictures.

"So," Earl started after she left, "what's going on? You seem a little distracted or something."

"Can't find my quilt," Nearly said, looking at Earl. "I don't know where it is."

"Well, it's gotta be here somewhere. Did you talk to Wilma or one of the nurses?"

"Nope. Haven't done that yet. I haven't been feeling that great."

"I'll go find Wilma and be right back, OK? Don't worry. We'll find it."

"Thanks, Earl. I need to find it. Can't believe I lost it."

The tension in his friend's voice circled around Earl's head as he walked to the desk. The quilt was about the only thing Nearly owned, and more importantly, his mother made it for him, to protect him. If it was the last good thing Earl ever did, he was going to find that quilt.

He saw Wilma standing in the hallway speaking rather sternly to a young female aide.

"You do not have to put up with that, Adelaide. Next time that happens, you tell me. Immediately." Wilma looked at Earl approaching. "117 and 119 need new bed sheets," she told the young woman, who managed a slight smile as she passed Earl.

"Mr. Johansen," Wilma stated. "How can I help you?"

Earl noticed for the first time that Wilma was wearing a name tag. It said "Evelyn Root." He wondered why he never noticed it before. Evelyn, Earl thought, looking at her and seeing if it fit. Nope. Still Wilma.

"My friend, Mr. Kelly …"

"Yes?" Wilma said with some impatience.

"He's missing something that belongs to him. It's his quilt."

"His quilt," Wilma echoed.

"Yes, the one his mother made for him."

"I know the quilt," she said. "And it's quite beautifully done, I might add."

Earl was surprised to hear her offer this kind gesture. In that moment he realized that Wilma, for all her rigid rules, did not miss a thing about the people in her care, patients or staff.

"Come with me," she said, and started down the hall to Nearly's room.

There wasn't much space to search. The quilt was not there. Wilma asked when Nearly last saw it.

"It was here yesterday when I went to lunch. I don't take it with me to lunch. I usually put it under my pillow if I leave my room."

"And when you came back from lunch, it wasn't here." Wilma was finishing the story. Earl felt helpless, hearing the tightness in Nearly's voice.

"Mr. Kelly," she said, "I will ask the staff to keep an eye out for it. Now, it might be difficult but I want you to try to relax."

"I'll be right back," Earl said to Nearly as he followed Wilma out into the hallway.

"I will ask the staff. There are a number of them who know what the quilt looks like," she said.

The quilt was unmistakable. It was a cream colored fabric with a black border. In the middle, also framed in black, a star—gold in the middle and out from that center, colors of autumn seemed to shoot to the tips, rusty browns, reds and yellows.

Earl suddenly brightened. "There's a picture of it. Would that help?"

"Well, yes, I suppose, if you have one."

Earl went in and reassured Nearly that he would return in a little while. "Why don't you rest your eyes, try to nap."

Then he left in search of Laurie.

It was overcast. The heat rose but was contained by the clouds that covered Campbell. The humidity increased with every block Earl walked. He went back to his house and called Marlene. There was no answer. He walked to Della's. Laurie had not been there since 11:30 when they had lunch. Earl removed his Cubs cap and scratched his head. *She's taking pictures somewhere,* he thought. Replacing his cap, he started walking, thinking he might go to the town line road. It was a ways but the walk would do him good.

Making his way through town, Earl turned the corner where the town hall stood. She was taking pictures of the old public works building. The brick on the building was in surprisingly good shape, but looked worn and dirty. One window, sealed up with plywood, had been broken earlier in the spring by either a rock thrown by a young Tommy Wilder or, if you believe Tommy Wilder, by a tree branch that suddenly snapped off in the wind and hit the window.

"Laurie!" Earl called out. Laurie turned, surprised.

"Hey!" she said, smiling. "What are you doing here? Did something happen?"

"No. Not really." Earl was a little out of breath. Instead of his slow, steady gait, he had been walking with some urgency. "I need to talk with you. Nearly lost his quilt."

"His quilt … did somebody take it?" Laurie's brow was furrowed. She sounded concerned.

"I don't know. But the folks at the VA are trying to look for it and I thought maybe they could see your picture."

"Oh! Sure!" Laurie said. She set her backpack on the ground, knelt in front of it and placed her camera inside. Then she took out the cardboard sleeve and looked through the photographs. Earl was about to tell her he would get the picture back to her by the end of the day when she stood up and said, "Got it. Let's go."

Laurie sat with Nearly in his room while Earl brought the photo to Wilma. Nearly was in his wheelchair wearing an old maroon robe over a black-and-gold Iowa Hawkeyes sweatshirt and sweatpants. His face still looked worn and worried.

"Were you out taking pictures?" Nearly asked.

"Yup, I was," Laurie responded. "I went over to the town hall and took a few."

"Y'know, they used to make announcements from that little building next to the town hall."

"Yeah, I heard about that," Laurie replied. "Doesn't look like the building's been used in a while."

"Probably not," Nearly said. "When Earl and me got back from overseas, I wanted to make my own announcement." Nearly smiled. "We had a few beers, I guess."

Even though Laurie had heard this story from Earl, she said, "So, what happened?"

"Well …" he paused, looking down and flexing his good foot. "Like I said, I guess we'd had a few beers. Earl must've been a little bit more sober 'cause he wouldn't do it. I thought it would be fun." He paused, then added, "Kinda regret that, I guess."

The disappointment in his voice almost made Laurie cry. She thought about other people's regrets. Her grandmother once said she regretted never taking that trip to London with her church group to see Elizabeth ascend the throne. Laurie's friend Carlos said he regretted not taking Fatima Aguilar to the spring dance. Her father wanted to be a photographer but left it as a passionate hobby in favor of a regular paycheck and benefits.

And here was Nearly who just wanted to say a few words to the citizens of Campbell.

Wilma and her staff had more to do than look for a quilt. Earl decided to stroll through the building. He tried to look casual as he quickly poked his head into open doors or walked along the hallway. Many of the people here were older than Earl, but the realization that some of them were his age had him hearing two words with each step he took: *Not yet … not yet.*

There was a patient in a wheelchair up ahead, slowly rolling down the hall. Earl wondered how hard it was to move yourself in one of those things. From all the times he pushed Nearly, he knew the chair itself was heavy. Never mind the person sitting in it who sometimes dragged his good foot on the floor. Suddenly, Earl stopped, squinted, and called out, "Excuse me …" The wheelchair kept rolling.

"Excuse me. Hey …" Earl said, walking a little faster. A quilt was draped over the back of the chair.

He caught up with the patient and grabbed on to the push handles. "Excuse me, hey …" he said again, stopping the chair and moving around to the front.

"What d'you want?" the man growled.

"Lars?" Earl said. "You're Lars Petersen, right?"

The ice-blue eyes flickered in recognition.

"So? What d'you want?"

"I'm Earl."

"I know who you are. Leave me alone."

Lars tried to move his wheelchair but Earl stopped him.

"Get out of my way!" Lars barked. "I didn't like you then and I don't like you now!"

Earl looked down at Lars. He had lost his hair and his scalp was dotted with age spots. Lars and Earl were the same age but had made different choices in life. One Sunday, Pastor Blomquist at the Lutheran church said that one could chose to walk with life or wrestle with it. It looked like Lars wrestled and, of course, lost.

"Give me the quilt," Earl said quietly.

Lars looked straight ahead and said nothing.

"Lars?"

"Forget it!" he snapped.

A tall, broad woman with skin the color of caramel approached. Her name tag said *Aisha Kombuta, nursing*. She was followed by Adelaide, the young woman Wilma had been speaking to in the hall when this whole thing started.

"What is going on here?" Nurse Kombuta said with concern laced in a lightly accented voice.

"This man is bothering me!" Lars said without looking directly at her.

"I am not bothering him," Earl said evenly. "Would you mind contacting Wil … uh … Miss Root? Evelyn Root, please."

Nurse Kombuta looked at Earl. "Adelaide, go get Ms. Root," she said to the young aide.

"I'm going to my room," Lars said, his hands on the wheels.

"Let's all go sit in the day room," Nurse Kombuta said calmly, taking control of Lars' chair.

After about ten minutes, during which Earl stood by the window and made small talk with the nurse, Wilma showed up.

"Thank you, Aisha," she said to the woman. She sat down next to where Lars was parked and placed her hand on the armrest of his wheelchair.

"Mr. Petersen, I need to ask you where you got this quilt."

Lars looked at no one and said nothing.

"Mr. Petersen?"

"Maybe it's mine," he said gruffly.

"Maybe it isn't," Earl said.

"Please, Mr. Johansen," Wilma said, holding up her hand. "Mr. Petersen, where did you get it?"

"Maybe I've always had it," Lars said. "Maybe it's … it's … a family what'cha call it …"

Earl rolled his eyes. He wanted to say: *You're old and you're sick and you're still picking on people, you pathetic bastard.* But, of course, he didn't. He was trusting Wilma to get to the bottom of it.

"I need to tell you that we have proof that this is most likely not your quilt," Wilma said. Her voice was steady and kind. "Please give me the quilt and we will not talk about it again."

"Damn Indian-lover," Lars muttered.

Wilma straightened as if an electric current ran up her back. "Pardon me? What did you say?"

Lars raised his torso as much as he could, put his face closer to hers and snarled, "I said goddamn *Indian*-lover!"

Wilma did not flinch. Her face showed no signs of what she might be thinking. Earl thought it looked as though her eyes were doing their best to bore holes into Lars' head. She stood, taking the quilt from the back of the chair. Placing herself directly in front of Lars, she said tersely, "This is a community, Mr. Petersen. We do not take things from one another. If you do not like it here, perhaps other arrangements can be made." Earl followed her as she left the day room and quickly walked down the hall.

"What would you say," Laurie asked, "if you could make an announcement?"

Nearly mused for a moment before responding. "I've been thinking about that 'cause Earl asked me that too. Do you like movies?"

"Sure," Laurie said.

"You ever seen *Harvey*?"

"I've heard of it but I haven't seen it."

"This guy, Elwood, his best friend is a six-foot-tall rabbit that no one else can see," Nearly said. "And people aren't very nice to Elwood, even though he's a really good guy." Shifting his weight in his chair, he continued.

"My memory isn't very good, but I still remember a line from that movie." Nearly closed his eyes and smiled. "He says … Elwood says … 'My mother told me in this world you must be oh so smart or oh so pleasant. I recommend pleasant.'"

As Laurie listened, wishing she could make this man's life better from now on, Wilma entered with her quick steps and the quilt in her arms.

The relief on Nearly's face when he was reunited with his quilt was worth every moment of effort. Laurie was beaming. Earl watched Nearly smooth the quilt over his lap.

Wilma simply gave it to him, telling him they found it. And after asking if there was anything else she might do, she went on her way.

Scraping the floor with a heavy chair as he brought it closer to Nearly, Earl sat down next to Laurie.

"You'll never guess who took it," Earl said.

"Probably Lars," Nearly responded absently, his big hands slowly, tenderly petting the quilt.

Genuinely surprised, Earl leaned back in his chair and looked at Nearly. "How did you know that?"

"Oh, I don't know," Nearly said. "He hasn't been very nice to me since he got here."

"You never said anything. I mean, you told me he was here, but …"

"Who's Lars?" Laurie asked.

Earl gave an abbreviated history of the Petersen boys and the various ways they bullied those they deemed different or weaker.

"And Lars ended up here." Earl concluded.

"Wow," Laurie said. "What are the odds?"

"Not too bad, I think," Nearly said. "I mean, he served in the Marines, and he never moved away so sooner or later … it's either here or the cemetery."

That Nearly was nearing the end of his road was something Laurie had stuffed into a closet, not wanting to think about it. Nearly's comment took the latch off the door.

****

A few bottles of Guinness stood in Earl's refrigerator behind a carton of milk and a package of cold cuts. The Guinness was for special friends, usually Nearly, or at the end of a day that felt like a week.

He was introduced to the dark beer with the beautiful foam by a guy he met in basic training. The training was, indeed, basic and quite brief as Earl remembered, and Jim Fitzgerald seemed to speak only of beer.

Some ten years older than Earl, Jim began each story with "When I was your age …" and ended each story with "Now we're talkin'!"

"When I was your age, I went to Ireland. The Irish, my friend, know beer," Jim stated. "The beer they have in the States is piss. You wanna real beer? Guinness!" he said with a glint in his eye. "Now we're talkin'!"

The evening came and Earl welcomed it. He poured the Guinness into a tall glass, grabbed the mail that had piled up, and sat down in his old, comfortable chair. With a contented sigh, he put his tired feet up on a little mismatched ottoman. Setting the beer on the end table he thought, *Nearly's missing quilt, his hospital stay, Laurie's trouble with her grandmother … I'm not used to this much excitement.* He took a healthy slug of Guinness.

Other than the bill from the power company, most of the mail was nothing important. Banks Dry Goods having a sale, O'Brien's Chinese restaurant advertising their Sunday buffet. There was a little booklet that said: *If Christ Had Not Come.* He resented the Jehovah's Witnesses coming to his door with this crap. If he wanted to know about what they believed and why, he would ask. At least he liked to think he would ask.

The phone rang.

Can't a man just sit and drink his beer without being interrupted?

He was tired and getting out of the chair required some effort. On his way over to the phone, he bent over to pick up what turned out to be a postcard under the kitchen table. There was a dull ache in his back causing him to groan a little as he straightened up.

"Hello?"

"Hey, Earl. It's me. Laurie!"

"Oh, well. Hello!" He looked at the clock. It was 7:35. "Is anything wrong?"

"Nope. Not at all. I wanted to ask you to join us—that'd be me *and* Aunt Marlene—for lunch tomorrow. Della's at 11:30." Energy and confidence carried her voice through the line.

"Tomorrow?" It was always nice seeing Laurie and he would certainly enjoy Marlene's company. But he wondered why they would invite him.

"I'm buying, Earl. A free lunch! C'mon, you can't pass that up!" Laurie joked.

"No, I guess not," Earl agreed. "I'll see you then."

Making his way back to the chair and his Guinness, he looked at the card he had picked up before answering the phone. It was from his brother, Mitchell. It said he was going to be in Campbell. *Have plans to stay at the Days Inn on the Interstate. Have rented a car. Will be good to see you.*

Earl thought for a second, what day is it? He looked at the postcard. The postmark was a little over two weeks ago. Mitchell would be here in two days.

That evening as he got up from the table to put his plate and glass in the sink, he glanced at Mitchell's book. He had not read it yet and hoped his brother wouldn't ask him about it. Earl was glad to have plans tomorrow.

There were promising yellow flowers on the tomato plant. It was planted late this year, given the cooler-than-normal May. A new neighbor a couple of doors down, a Mexican fellow named Ernesto something-or-other, told Earl he had planted a salsa garden—jalapeños, tomatoes, cilantro. Earl figured his tomato plant and his lettuce made up his BLT garden. He'd have to buy the bacon.

Early morning was the best time to water the plants. Watching the rainbow in the mist of the spray from the hose, thoughts ran around in Earl's head as if in a relay race. Mitchell's impending visit. *What would they talk about? He could tell him about Laurie and her pictures. Last night she sounded like she had something specific she wanted to say. What might that be? And Nearly. He wasn't looking so good lately but maybe the return of his quilt helped. Maybe Mitchell would like to stop by and say hi to Nearly. Pretty sure he would. When was the last time Mitchell had been here? Earl couldn't remember. Maybe fifteen years?*

Earl finally shook his head, as if by doing so these thoughts would stop or run off to some other part of his brain.

****

Laurie and Marlene were already seated when Earl arrived.

"Hey, Earl!" Laurie said brightly. "I got our usual spot."

It was the same booth they seemed to sit in whenever they met at Della's. He felt somewhat uncomfortable hearing her say *our usual spot* in front of Marlene, but he wasn't sure quite why. Surely no one would ever suspect an eighteen-year-old to have the slightest interest in an old man, other than in a grandfatherly way.

Marlene was about to get up to greet him.

"No, no, don't get up," he said cheerfully as he positioned himself on the vinyl seat across from the two girls. "Hard enough sliding in and out of these things." He paused and looked around. "I don't see Della."

The menus were examined as if something unexpected might

have been added since the last visit. A woman wearing a white short-sleeved blouse, black slacks and a waist apron appeared. She had worked at Della's for at least fifteen years. Her name was stitched above her pocket: *Trudy*. Trudy's life story was written on her face with a multitude of fine lines.

"Hey, Earl," she rasped, her voice low, torn up by too many cigarettes and late-night whiskey sours.

"Trudy," said Earl, nodding. "What's new? You aren't usually here on weekdays are you?"

"Nothin' gets by you." She smiled with crooked, nicotine-stained teeth. The smile disappeared as a look of concern came over her face. "Andy took a turn last night. Della's at the hospital." Hardly missing a beat, she perked up and said, "So, folks. What'll you have?"

Marlene ordered a grilled chicken salad, Laurie the grilled cheese.

"Turkey sandwich," Earl said.

"You want coleslaw, fries or chips?" Trudy asked.

"Fries," Earl said and then suddenly changed his mind saying, "Wait a sec ... coleslaw."

Taking the menus, Trudy deadpanned, "You're a wild one, Earl."

Marlene and Laurie smiled at this. Earl shook his head.

"One of these days I'll order a salad. That'll show her!" he joked. Folding his hands together on top of the table he looked at Laurie and said, "Well?"

"Well what?" Laurie smiled. Earl could have sworn he saw Marlene roll her eyes.

"I want you to know, I had nothing to do with this," Marlene said to him.

"But you think it's a good idea," Laurie said as if finishing the thought.

"I don't believe I ever said it was a good idea," Marlene said firmly. "I said I appreciated that you wanted to do this for Nearly."

Earl sat there, waiting. He didn't want to interrupt them and figured that, sooner or later, they would get around to telling him what this idea was and how Nearly might be involved.

Laurie shifted a bit and leaned forward.

"I have a great idea. I think we should steal Nearly for a day."

Earl blinked. *Steal Nearly? What was she talking about?*

"Do you mean sign him out with a day pass and go to the movies or something?"

"Nope. Well, OK, maybe we sign him out or whatever but then …"

She smiled broadly at him. Earl waited.

"… then we let him make his announcement."

Earl looked over at Marlene, who was looking neutrally at her grandniece.

"What?" he said finally. "Do you mean … oh, I don't think that's …"

Earl was trying not to say the first thing that popped into his head: *Are you nuts?*

He took a deep breath.

"Laurie, I know you've taken a liking to Nearly. I mean, he's my best friend. But this is …"

"No, no it isn't …" Laurie jumped in. "I've got it all figured out. At least I *will* have it all figured out, but I'm gonna need your help."

Earl sat back. He could see that this must be tied to that unfulfilled dream discussion they had in this very booth. He knew if they sat there and talked this through, she would end up disappointed, but in his mind, a disaster would be averted.

"Laurie …" Earl said.

"Just hang on a sec. I gotta pee." Marlene got up and Laurie slid out of the booth and quickly walked to the restroom. Earl looked at Marlene.

"What in the world is she thinking?" Earl asked.

"Earl, she's young," Marlene said, as if that explained

everything. "And she has taken such a liking to Nearly. And to you."

"Maybe she could buy him something," Earl said helpfully, "or give him one of her photos. He'd like that. But trying to get into that old building and have him say who knows what?"

"I know," Marlene said. "I know."

They sat there in silence as a few seconds ticked by.

"There is something very sweet about what she wants to do," Marlene finally said. "I mean, I'm not one for breaking the rules—seems to me that was your department when we were kids."

Earl found himself suppressing a smile. His childhood would have been dull without Nearly. Sometimes their plans worked, sometimes not. But it was fun.

"Just listen to her."

"I'll do my best."

When Laurie returned she laid out her plan. It was a jumble of words, each one buoyed by her energy. He asked questions that at first were meant to tamp down Laurie's enthusiasm and help her understand—gently—that perhaps this wasn't the best idea. But as Earl asked the questions, he felt himself getting that tingle up his spine, the same feeling he had as a kid every time he and Nearly were about to color outside the lines. Suddenly he became aware that he was thinking about Nearly—a good man, a good friend—and the questions asked were to ensure the plan would succeed.

"Look, I'm not agreeing to anything," Earl said. "But ..." and here he paused and looked directly into Laurie's blue eyes, "I will walk over to the building with you and take a look."

Laurie almost knocked over her Diet Coke, reaching over to grab Earl's arm.

"Yes! I knew you'd want to!"

"I'm not into this yet," he said, adding the most adult phrase he could think of: "We'll see."

After lunch, the three of them started strolling over to the town hall area. As much as Earl wanted a cigarette, he knew Marlene and Laurie would disapprove. The pack stayed snug in his pocket.

"Mitchell's coming into town tomorrow," Earl said, making conversation.

"Really?" Marlene said. "I hope I can see him. I always liked your brother."

"I was thinking maybe we could all have lunch or dinner while he's here."

"Wonderful! How long will he be staying?" she asked.

Earl hesitated. Was there anything in that card saying how long his brother was going to be here?

"I don't know. I don't think he said how long."

"Why don't we have dinner at my house?" Marlene suggested.

Earl thought that was generous and told her so. He volunteered to bring a salad and some bread. The Hy-Vee recently expanded their bakery to include some loaves that at least looked home-baked.

The public works building was a small, perfectly square structure. The three cement stairs leading up to the landing were cracked, the corner of the second step crumbling. The door was weathered solid oak. Earl looked at it. There was a padlock on a flimsy hinge. A sturdy screwdriver would pop that off. The doorknob jiggled but it did not turn. Locked from the inside. It was a skeleton key lock and would be easy to open. He just needed to remember to bring the right tools, a thin-blade screwdriver or stiff piece of wire. *There's a reason they don't use skeleton locks anymore*, thought Earl. *Too easy to pick.*

"It's locked up tight, isn't it?" Laurie said, doing her best to ward off disappointment.

"No, not really," Earl said.

Laurie smiled.

****

The aroma of a Big Mac, a Filet-O-Fish and two large orders of fries filled the hallway outside of Nearly's room. It wasn't exactly allowed at the VA but no one enforced the restriction.

"Thanks for dinner," Nearly said, taking another bite out of the sandwich.

Earl nodded, his mouth full of fries.

"I think they were having beef stroganoff in the dining room." Nearly paused, chewing. "Fish sandwich is better." Another pause. He continued: "I don't know about eating beef anymore. When I come back, I'm gonna be a vegetarian."

Nearly had a vault full of things he'd been thinking about, saving for years. Now his thoughts came out as if the editors in his brain had been laid off, no guards on duty.

"You planning on coming back?" Earl asked reaching for his iced tea.

"Sure. You?"

"I don't know." Earl figured that there might be an afterlife, another swing at getting it right. Or maybe dead is dead. Whichever one it was, he'd find out. He decided to change the subject.

"Mitchell's coming for a visit. He gets here tomorrow."

"Oh, yeah?" Nearly brightened. "We sure gave him a hard time. Nice kid."

"Well, the 'kid,' as you say, is retiring from teaching. He's on some kind of book tour."

"How was the book?" Nearly asked, grabbing a few fries.

Earl looked at Nearly blankly. "I don't know. He sent it to me. I haven't read it."

Nearly narrowed his eyes and leaned toward Earl.

"Jeez, Earl … I don't know. He's your brother … went to all the trouble of writing a whole book."

Earl suddenly felt terrible.

"Guess I know what I'm doing tonight," he mumbled.

Nearly nodded. There was a minute or two with the sounds

of distant televisions and radios, soft footsteps of nurses and aides in the hallway.

Nearly said, "You'll come back. We'll have a great time all over again."

****

Once at home he sat down in his chair and reluctantly picked up his brother's book. He figured he should at least skim it.

When he finally turned off the light, it was 1:30 a.m.

The book was quite good, with places where Earl chuckled out loud. A couple of times he stopped reading, looked at the photograph of his brother, and shook his head in amazement. This was as good as the books by that Maupin fellow.

He had suspected there was something going on between Mitchell and Johnny Coldwell. Chapter seven confirmed it. Even though Mitchell protected Johnny by referring to him in the story as "Bud," the description of the boy was so clear, Earl could still see him standing at the door asking if Mitchell was home. That chapter and several other pages made Earl feel a little uncomfortable.

One short section in particular struck Earl as not only unfair but also untrue. It was a lightly veiled description of a woman Earl was sure must be Marlene. Like the character in the book, the summer after high school, Marlene helped coach the girls' softball team at the junior high school. The way Mitchell described this woman and her relationship with the other coach made her sound, well, homosexual or something. He made a mental note to ask Mitchell about this particular passage and if he was referring to Marlene Goodhue. Could this be?

Mitchell had been kind to Earl, and loving to Verna, to whom the book was dedicated. A few people in Campbell did not fare quite so well. Their father got what he deserved in these pages, as did their mother. He remembered his grandmother saying that if people would like to be remembered well after they die, they need to behave a little better while they live.

Late the next morning, he was outside watering the geraniums and impatiens in the window boxes when he heard a car approaching. A silver Ford Escort pulled up. The man who exited the small car was as lanky and tall as when they were teenagers, but carried himself with a little stiffness. Earl envied that his brother inherited their father's height. Earl, on the other hand, was built more like their maternal grandmother, short and solid.

"Earl!" Mitchell smiled broadly as he walked toward his brother. Earl thought he noticed a slight limp. If their grandmother were present, she would have said, "Mitchell's got a little hitch in his git-along."

"Well, there you are!" Earl responded, smiling. The two men embraced in a brief, awkward imitation of a hug.

"You look good, Earl," Mitchell said politely.

"You too. How was the trip?"

"Oh, not bad. You know." There was an uneasy pause. "Driving wasn't bad at all, not even the construction."

"Oh, was there construction? Where?" Earl asked. *Another good reason to not travel,* he thought.

"On I-35 near Ames. It seems they are always working on that section of freeway."

"Well," Earl said, putting his hand lightly on his brother's back, "come on in, I'll show you around. That'll take about three minutes." They both chuckled.

Once they got inside the tiny house and engaged in more small talk, Earl was relieved to see it was getting near lunchtime.

"Why don't we walk over to Della's for lunch."

"Della's! It's still open?"

"Oh my, yes," Earl said. "And Della is still there."

Mitchell looked at the ground.

"Would you mind too much if we drove to Della's?"

"No, that's all right." It was a fine summer's day, but Earl felt that he needed to be a good host. If Mitchell wanted to drive, then they'd drive.

As the two men got in the rental car and started off for the diner, Mitchell said, "I think the last time I was at Della's was after Gram's funeral. What was that—ten years now?"

"Almost fifteen—1981," Earl replied. He felt some irritation that Mitchell didn't remember when Verna died. When Mitchell moved away from Campbell, the man never looked back.

The pauses in their conversation were not comfortable for Earl. He hoped he didn't run out of things to say.

"Well, I was thinking maybe we'd run over to the cemetery at some point. Oh, and we've been invited to dinner tomorrow night. Remember Marlene Goodhue?"

"Oh, sure."

"Well, I told her you'd be in town. Her grandniece is visiting too. A nice young lady, I think she's taken a real shine to Nearly. He's been invited to the dinner too, if he's up to it."

****

Nearly felt better than he had in a long time. Jack, his favorite aide, helped him get to the shower, assisted him in getting dressed and settled him in his wheelchair.

"Your chariot, my man," Jack smiled. "Anything else I can do for you, sir?"

"Nope, I think that's it," Nearly replied. "Oh, wait. Would you hand me my quilt?"

To say that Jack was a big man was an understatement. His well-muscled body was evident even under his scrubs. The quilt looked tiny in his large, dark hands as he gently folded it and handed it to Nearly.

"I'll get you out the door, but once you're in the hallway, you're on your own," Jack said, wheeling Nearly out the door. He added, "That's a nice quilt."

"My mom made it," Nearly said.

"My momma quilts too. Nothin' like handmade."

"Guess not."

Jack stopped pushing once they cleared the doorway. "There y'go, man. Have a good day. Call if you need anything."

"Thanks, Jack."

Nearly wheeled himself slowly down the hall. He had lost track of time but even that didn't bother him. It's not like he was doing anything. All he knew for sure was that he was here on this planet, still breathing, still able to roll along the hallway and stop to say hello to the others who were waiting for whatever came next. Occasionally, he could even make room for some compassionate thoughts about Lars but knew it was best to steer clear of him.

Sitting at a table, the two brothers chatted amiably over lunch. Della stopped by to refill their coffee. It seemed to Earl that her shoulders drooped a little.

"And who is this handsome man?" Della said. Everyone laughed softly.

Mitchell stood and gave Della a light hug. "Della. Good to see you."

"Where the hell've you been, anyway?" she said. Before Mitchell could say anything, Della went on: "Oh, I know. You're quite the well-known writer now. My friend Marguerite sent me an article from some newspaper. Sent it 'cause it mentioned Campbell." Della put her hand on her hip. "Imagine my surprise to see a photo of Mitch Johansen!"

Earl winced. Very few people had ever called Mitchell "Mitch."

"I'm here for a few days, visiting," Mitchell responded.

"If you came earlier, I would've missed you," Della said. Looking at Earl, she continued: "I was at the hospital. Lord have mercy, I've lost track of how many doctors Andy has looking at him."

"Trudy tells me that Andy took a turn," Earl said. "Sorry to hear that."

Della sighed and slowly shook her head. "Thanks. It won't be long now, and I'm thinking that's all right."

Earl nodded, thinking that a massive heart attack or stroke that takes you out is the way to go. Or just not waking up. This long exit stuff is not pretty. Nobody but life insurance companies benefits from keeping people alive past their expiration date. Probably the pharmaceutical folks too.

"You boys enjoy your time. Mitchell? Don't be a stranger."

Della left to chat up the next table.

"I was thinking we might stop over to the VA and say hey to Nearly," Earl said.

"That sounds fine," Mitchell responded. "How is he doing?"

Earl rubbed his chin. "Well, OK, I guess. They got him connected up to some oxygen, and sometimes he just rambles a bit. But he's still here. I sure hope he's going to want to go to dinner tomorrow night. He'd sure enjoy something like that."

Mitchell nodded. After a pause, he said, "Listen, Earl ..."

The hair on the back of Earl's neck stood on end.

When they were boys, Earl had a summer job cleaning the movie theater. Even with the sticky floors and the litter, Earl liked the job. When people sat watching a movie, they weren't aware of things like dimes and quarters falling out of their pockets. After his first night cleaning the theater, he had collected a dollar and forty-five cents in change. He went to sign out with the theater manager and handed him the change.

"Oh, no. You get to keep that, son. Wallets—well, wallets have to be turned in, but small change on the floor? Finders keepers!"

A dollar and forty-five cents! This was going to be a good job.

Earl found change on the floor most nights. He put it in a jar in his closet, saving up for a new bike.

Coming home from baseball practice one day, Earl went into his room. Mitchell was sitting on the bed looking anxious.

He broke the news to Earl that their father came in drunk, threw stuff around and found the jar. He took it.

That day, from that moment on, the way Mitchell started to tell bad news to his brother was, "Listen, Earl ... "

Earl looked at his brother. "Let's get the check and we can start over to the VA."

"So?" Earl said as soon as they were both on the sidewalk outside of Della's.

Mitchell lifted his face to the sun for a moment.

"I have ..." Mitchell hesitated. Earl could only hear the word cancer at the end of that sentence. Somehow it was never: *I have a lot of money and I don't know what to do with it so I think I'll give it to you.*

" ... a bad hip. It's osteoarthritis. I've been putting off having the surgery for a while now but it's getting to be a problem."

Earl felt a simultaneous wash of relief and concern.

"Well, I was thinking we could stroll over to the VA, but would you rather drive?" Earl used his two good legs to go almost everywhere. He never thought it might be a problem for others to take a pleasant walk, but here was his own brother, possibly in pain.

"I think so, yes. I'm missing so many of these beautiful days. I think that's what helped me decide to just have the surgery."

As they drove the short distance to the VA, Earl asked, "So when are you going to have this done, this operation?"

"Soon. I'm going to see the surgeon when I return from this trip. The surgery will most likely be scheduled in September."

"Seems like a difficult operation, going into a hip like that. Do you have anyone to take care of you, y'know, help you out?" Earl hesitated to ask this last question. It seemed too personal. And what if the answer was, *Well, brother, I thought I might stay with you.*

"Oh, I'm fine. I have many good friends," Mitchell said reassuringly. "And a couple of them have already had one or both hips worked on!" he added with a chuckle.

I wonder if this is from sitting too much, all of these hip problems, Earl thought. *My hips are fine.*

"A guy I know, Mel, said I'd be up and around in no time," Mitchell said.

"I'm glad you have folks to help you out. You'll let me know, right?"

"Of course."

****

Nearly sat alone, looking out the large window in the day room. The VA had worn furniture and people in various states of decline, but its windows were big and clean. Looking at the trees outside, he thought he could hear the wind moving through them, making the leaves flutter. But what he was hearing was the soft hiss of his oxygen. *What day was it?*

"There he is!" Nearly heard a familiar voice. He turned his wheelchair.

"Hey," Nearly said.

"Brought a visitor," Earl said.

"Hi, Nearly."

"Mitchell," Nearly smiled. The two men shook hands. "Good to see you, man. You got tall."

Mitchell smiled. "I guess so."

Earl said, "It's a nice day out there—a little breezy but nice. Thought we might go outside."

They walked down the hallway, Earl pushing Nearly in the wheelchair, Mitchell walking with a slight limp. Passing the nurses station, Wilma looked up over the frame of her glasses.

"Mr. Johansen," she said. Earl was worried that she was going to start in about the smoking. Instead she gave him a nod and—was that a smile?—and said, "Good to see you."

"I dunno, Earl," Nearly teased as the fresh summer air touched his face. "I think she likes you."

Earl ignored Nearly's comment, guiding the chair down the ramp.

"I never realized these grounds were so beautiful," Mitchell said, sitting down stiffly on the bench under an enormous old oak tree.

"It's pretty," Nearly said. "Is it pretty where you live? I mean, where do you live? I guess I don't know."

"I live in St. Paul," Mitchell replied. "And, yes, it's pretty where I live."

"That's good," Nearly said. "Sometimes I think people like to talk about pretty places but they don't sit in them much."

Mitchell looked at him. "You're quite the philosopher, Nearly."

Nearly nodded his head.

The next day, the two brothers enjoyed a leisurely breakfast at Della's, a drive out to the cemetery to pay their respects to Verna, and lunch at a restaurant Mitchell heard of that had opened recently fifteen miles outside of Campbell.

"It was reviewed in the *New York Times*!" he exclaimed.

The portions were small with fancy designs on the plate made out of cream or salad dressing. Earl wasn't sure. Mitchell was practically swooning over his salad of beets, grilled chicken, goat cheese and toasted walnuts on a bed of field greens. The poultry was no doubt raised at a fancy hotel for chickens, Earl thought. As he took his first bite of a turkey burger with some kind of sauce on it that seemed spicy, he hoped Marlene would have what he called "three-piles": meat, vegetable, potato. As he took his second bite, he longed for ketchup and mustard.

Earl was glad for the break when Mitchell went back to the motel to freshen up. He was equally grateful that this evening it wouldn't be just the two of them. As much as Earl wished they were close, the truth was, they weren't. That thought brought him a twinge of sadness. Mitchell was a nice guy though, Earl thought. Thanks to Verna. God knows it had nothing to do with their parents.

He remembered talking to Verna about a year before she passed. She seemed to be in the mood to talk about her daughter, the family. It was a topic she usually avoided.

"You and Mitchell did OK," she said. "I'm proud of both of you."

"We had you, Gram. Sure didn't have anyone else."

"No, you didn't. Sorry about that," Verna confirmed. "But you two are made of good stuff."

When Earl and Mitchell pulled up to the VA, Nearly was already sitting outside, dressed once again in his charcoal gray corduroys, a white shirt and black bolo tie with an agate pendant. He lifted his hand as a wave to them.

After settling Nearly into the front seat with his oxygen and his quilt, the two brothers struggled to get the wheelchair folded. Earl and Mitchell did their best to wrestle the chair into the trunk but it wouldn't fit.

"Let's just put it in the back seat with me," Earl said, trying to catch his breath. "There's room."

The scent of charcoal starting on a grill wafted to the front of Marlene's house as the three men approached. There was hope for food that felt comfortable to Earl. He knew Marlene wouldn't try any of that fancy stuff. That just wasn't her.

They were greeted warmly by Marlene, who walked them around to the back to avoid the few stairs up to the front door. Mitchell and Earl bumped Nearly and his wheelchair over the threshold and into the porch, where Earl had enjoyed his first dinner with Marlene and had been introduced to Laurie.

The grill was just outside the porch. Laurie stood next to it wearing an apron with the Iowa Hawkeye logo emblazoned in the middle.

"Hi, Nearly! Hey, Earl!" she called out cheerfully.

"Look at you, tending the coals," Earl said, walking toward her.

"I've never done this before. Aunt Marlene thinks I can handle it," she said with confidence.

There was a round metal tower about a foot high standing in the middle of the grill.

"Oh, it's one of those starter things," Earl commented. He had never seen one. Most people just piled up the briquettes, soaked them with lighter fluid and—poof! Barbeque à la Kingsford.

"Isn't it great?" Laurie answered. Marlene walked up to her grandniece.

The chimney was smoking but the pieces of charcoal on the top were still untouched by the fire.

"I think you have a little time before the grilling starts," she said. "Come on in and meet Earl's brother."

When they walked into the porch, Laurie gave Nearly a hug.

"Hey," Nearly said by way of greeting. It occurred to Earl that perhaps Nearly didn't remember her name. He thought bringing him here was a good idea but seeing him sitting there in his wheelchair, hooked up to his oxygen and looking a little pale, Earl had doubts.

"Laurie, this is my brother, Mitchell," Earl said.

Mitchell and Laurie extended their hands to one another and both said "Nice to meet you" at about the same time.

"She takes pictures," Nearly said. "They're real nice too."

"And now I have some of you!" Laurie laughed. Nearly nodded absently.

Marlene had set out some cheese and crackers. She had an ice chest containing soft drinks and beer.

"Does anyone want wine?"

"Do you have red?" Mitchell asked.

"I do," Marlene answered. "A friend of mine from California visits me once a year and always brings about five bottles of various reds and a few whites." She chuckled and shook her head. "I end up giving many of them away, but there are a few left. Come and take a look. You can have your pick."

Earl watched his brother walk off toward the kitchen with Marlene.

"This is nice," Nearly said, looking around. "You don't have to share your drink with the bugs."

Earl smiled. Nearly was right. It was nice to sit in a screen porch. The sun didn't beat down on your neck, a pleasant breeze drifted through, and—as Nearly said—no bugs. Earl thought maybe he would add a porch to his house too. Couldn't be that hard to build. His didn't need to be very big.

Laurie was standing closest to the ice chest.

"What can I get you, Nearly?" she said. "There's beer and, um … Coke, regular and diet …"

"Got any water?"

"I can get a glass for you. Earl? Want anything from the cooler?"

"Well, I guess I'll have a beer, but let me go get the water for Nearly. You sit down," he offered.

"I'm already up," Laurie protested.

"And you should sit down for a second," Earl said, getting up from the small sofa. "You're gonna be out there grilling any minute and you'll be standing for a while."

As Earl approached the kitchen, he heard Marlene's voice followed by Mitchell's. He stopped.

"I'm worried that he has the wrong idea and I feel terrible."

"Better to tell him. It might be a little uncomfortable, Marlene, but I know he'd understand. He's a good guy."

Who's a good guy? Earl thought. *What is he talking about?* Perplexed by what he heard (as well as slightly embarrassed by his eavesdropping), he took a few steps back then started walking again and called out as he approached, "Marlene, could I get a glass of water for Nearly?" By the time he finished his question, he had entered the kitchen. Earl smiled and pretended to not notice the static in the air or the slight reddening in his brother's cheeks. Marlene had her back to him, reaching in to a cupboard.

"Sure, Earl." she sounded nervous. "I … I should have

thought about that." She filled the glass with water from the tap. "Here you are. Anyone else want water?" she smiled.

"Not for me," Mitchell said with a bit too much of a cheerful lilt. "I have this lovely glass of zinfandel—a perfect match for the burger!"

Conversation stopped momentarily in an uncomfortably pregnant pause.

"Well, shall we go back to the porch?" Marlene said in an unusually high voice as she extended her arm toward the doorway.

Whatever tension there was followed them out of the kitchen and then, once on the porch, floated out through the screen. Earl watched Marlene giving Laurie a lesson in grilling. Since he couldn't hear them, it was like watching a pantomime.

She was a good teacher. The burgers brought to the dining room table were delicious—done to perfection. Marlene opened a jar of homemade dill pickles and put them alongside the lettuce, mayo, grilled onions, and—thank God—ketchup and mustard. Earl was pleased to see that his salad fit right in with the beautiful spread.

Mitchell was conversing with Laurie, asking her questions about where she was from and what she might want to do in the future. Earl was noticing that Nearly did not eat much. He had taken a small piece of his burger and placed it in a large cup-like piece of lettuce with the other condiments on top. It was odd but Earl did not want to draw attention to it.

Following dinner, they all went out to the porch again. Marlene served freshly baked cookies and coffee.

"Oh, chocolate chip," Nearly said, holding the cookie like a communion wafer for all to see. "My favorite."

"Me too," Laurie said. "Have they always been your favorite?"

"I guess there was a time my mom made ginger ones. Those were good too."

Small conversations followed about baking: who baked, what

they baked and how sad it was that small towns like Campbell no longer had a bakery. They had a section of a grocery store that was referred to as a bakery, but it wasn't really a bakery. Folks still missed the Main Street Bakery. Murray and Harriet Anderson ran it for more than 40 years—the two of them there at 3:00 in the morning. By 6:00 there was no better place to be than standing near the Andersons' store, the aroma of freshly baked bread, cookies and pies floating in the air. *That* was a bakery.

Earl could feel that the light breeze had become weighted with water. It would be a humid day tomorrow.

Nearly leaned over to Earl, whispering.

Earl stood up and unlocked the brakes on Nearly's chair.

"Gotta visit the head," Nearly announced.

"Can I help?" Mitchell offered.

"I'll let you know," Earl smiled.

The hallway was narrow and the wheelchair barely fit. Earl turned it around and walked slowly, backward. He parked it in the doorway, giving himself enough room to maneuver around to the front. Nearly put one hand on the arm of the chair and the other around Earl's neck. Earl nudged the chair back a little. Slowly, the two men got into the bathroom.

"Uh, Earl?" Nearly said. "I'm gonna need you to hang around so I don't fall down when I get up."

"When you get up? Aren't you gonna stand?"

"Nope. Easier to sit."

Earl turned his back while Nearly sat. Since when did a man sit when he took a leak? Of course, Nearly doesn't stand so well anymore so it made a certain amount of sense. Of all the humiliations that awaited him, Earl placed this near the top: having to be helped in the bathroom. Nearly was already there. Sadness filled Earl, but instead of feeling a tightness in his chest, as he had on other occasions, he felt it expand. He would do anything for Nearly.

While Nearly and Earl were out of earshot, Laurie turned to

her great-aunt and Mitchell. "I have something I wanted to talk to you about."

"Oh, Laurie," Marlene sighed, "don't drag Mitchell into this!"

"Why not?"

"Drag me into what?" Mitchell said.

"Nothing," Marlene said, looking at Laurie. "It's nothing, and Laurie was mistaken."

Laurie glared at Marlene. "I am *not* mistaken." There was an uncomfortable pause.

"As my brother might say: the horse is out of the barn," Mitchell said. "You may as well tell me."

Laurie told him the story Earl had relayed about coming home from the war, Nearly's disappointment that he carried to this day, and her own plan to take Nearly to the old public works building so that his dream could be fulfilled.

"Earl and I have already been there. Getting in is a piece of cake!"

"What if someone catches you?" Mitchell asked.

"So what? What are they going to do? Throw two old men and a juvie in jail? I don't think so."

Mitchell rubbed the back of his neck. He knew this enthusiasm. Some of his students had it. It was second nature to him, a professor, to challenge her, the student. "Think about this, then—and I'm only saying it because I think it is best to consider every angle, every possible thing that might go wrong."

Laurie sat forward in her chair, a tennis player waiting for the ball to be served.

"Nearly is in a wheelchair. It took some effort to get him over a small threshold," Mitchell said this with kindness. Laurie lobbed the ball back in his court.

"There are only a few steps, and between the four of us I know we can do it."

"The four of us!" Marlene sat up a little straighter.

"Fine. Whatever. Earl and I can do this without you, you know." Laurie looked at her aunt and then back at Mitchell.

The look Marlene gave her grandniece said *you should be grateful we are not alone, young lady.* Instead, she said, "None of us—Earl included—are spring chickens. This is not to be taken lightly. Nearly is not at all well."

"That's right, Nearly isn't well and that's *exactly* why I think we need to do this," Laurie said. "And Earl is fine, by the way."

Mitchell looked down at his shoes and said nothing.

Frustrated, Laurie got up and walked toward the door. She stopped and turned before she got there. Looking at Marlene she said, "You know what my gramma does? She talks about *all* the stuff she was gonna do." The word "all" turned into a sustained note, hanging in the air before the sentence could be completed.

"Muriel did plenty," Marlene said quietly but firmly.

"Maybe. But she didn't go to London. And she didn't finish her degree."

Marlene sighed and slumped a little. She had heard these same regrets from her sister. Laurie kept going.

"Let's see. Didn't enter anything at the fair when you were both in 4-H. Didn't learn how to play the freakin' accordion that sits there in the corner whenever she goes through this long list of what she didn't do!" Laurie crossed her arms in front of her chest. "I hear this probably twice a month, the list of stuff she *didn't do.* But we're *here* and we can help Nearly do this."

"And I think we should," Earl said, smiling. Surprised, everyone looked over at him as he rolled Nearly back into the room.

"Do what?" Nearly said weakly, trying to look over his shoulder at Earl.

Earl parked Nearly and sat in the chair across from him. Marlene, Mitchell and Laurie formed the rest of the circle.

"Well, Laurie here has an idea. A surprise. And at first I thought it wasn't so great."

Nearly looked at Laurie.

"My birthday is in December," he said.

Laurie looked at Earl and then back at Nearly. Hesitantly, she replied, "OK."

"Can't be for my birthday then," Nearly added.

Laurie laughed, reaching over and touching Nearly's arm. "No, no, it's not for your birthday!"

"'Course I guess we could celebrate it early. Y'never know," Nearly said. He gave her a crooked smile and added, "Life is short."

Marlene got up suddenly and asked Earl to help her round up the dishes and get them into the kitchen.

"We'll be back," Earl said to Nearly.

"Oh, OK. Well, we'll try to stay out of trouble while you're gone," Nearly replied, winking at Laurie. Mitchell watched them as they left the room.

Once in the kitchen, Marlene's voice was just a click above a whisper.

"I'm sorry to sound like this, Earl, but are you out of your mind?" She stood looking directly at Earl with her left hand on her hip and her right one straight-arming the counter. "Are you *really* going to go through with this?"

Earl suddenly felt as he did when he was questioned by his grandmother about six missing cookies he had taken for him and Nearly to share.

But he wasn't on that end of life; he was on this one. The only sure thing was that every person present tonight would eventually leave this world. Nearly was most likely going to be the first one out.

"Well, sure," Earl said, standing straighter. "Yes, I am going to go through with it."

"Earl," Marlene started, "Please don't let my niece —"

"I'm not letting your niece do anything, Marlene. And, yes, at first I thought it was the most harebrained idea I ever heard. But then I remembered all the crazy, harebrained things Nearly and I used to do and y'know what?"

Marlene continued to look at Earl without answering him.

"Best times of my life," he said, hoping she didn't notice the slight rasp in his voice.

Marlene's body relaxed. She dropped her arms to her side and looked down for a moment. The kindness returned to her voice. "You two have been best friends ever since I've known you."

Earl stood there wondering why she was stating the obvious. He felt a little pissed off, too. He was a grown man, and if he wanted to risk getting in trouble again then it's up to him, isn't it?

"It's just … Laurie …" Marlene continued with some pauses. "I love my grandniece … she has always needed to fix things for people, make their lives better."

"Nothing wrong with that," Earl interjected.

"No, but she gets these ideas …" Marlene hesitated. "And I know this is about her father, this focus on following your dreams, unfulfilled dreams, and so on."

Earl rubbed the back of his neck. He didn't care why Laurie wanted to do this for Nearly. It didn't matter. If his best friend was willing, so was he.

"I'm pretty sure Laurie has told Nearly what the plan is by now," he said. "I think I'll go in and find out what he wants to do." He walked out of the kitchen.

When he entered the porch, Nearly looked as if he could stand up and walk out the door under his own power. He gave Earl a smile.

"Guess what Laurie wants to do," he said. Earl had not heard this much lift, this much excitement in his voice for a long time.

"I think I know," Earl said. "So, are you up for it?"

"Yeah, I am," Nearly said. "We're gonna go tonight."

"Tonight?" Earl said, surprised.

"Tonight," Laurie said not even trying to contain her excitement. "That's the plan!"

"I never know if I'm gonna be here, but I'm here now so let's go," Nearly said, his hands ready to roll his chair forward.

"Are you sure about this?" Mitchell said to his brother.

Earl hesitated for only a few seconds. He was thinking about the padlock that hung on the door to the public works building.

"Marlene?" he called back to the kitchen, "do you have a decent screwdriver?"

The days were still long even though they were well past the summer solstice. It wasn't until after 8:00 when the sun slowly began to make its trek to the horizon. Marlene did, in fact, have a decent small flat-blade screwdriver. To Earl's wonder, she had a workbench that made his heart skip a beat—complete with tools, most of them Craftsman. Opening up a large slate-gray metal toolbox, she handed him a flashlight, saying sternly, "You'll need this."

"Good thinking."

"I want you to know I am going along with this in order to protect my niece. I want to be on the record as saying this is a ridiculous idea."

"Duly noted," said Earl. He paused, then added, " I'll need a hammer too. Oh, and a thin piece of wire if you have it."

Marlene's house was not that far from the center of town. Earl, Laurie and Nearly made their way down the street, the moist evening air clinging to their skin. Anyone in Campbell looking out their windows would see Earl Johansen and that girl who is visiting Marlene Goodhue pushing that old Indian in a wheelchair.

Since Mitchell had his hip problem, he and Marlene said they'd get there in the car. Both Marlene and Mitchell made it clear that they would not be a part of actually breaking into the building.

"Sorry, Earl," Mitchell said. "This is already a little more than I thought would happen on my visit."

****

Earl walked up the three steps to the door of the building. Laurie waited, standing next to Nearly on the sidewalk. Grinley's Funeral Home was across the street, a brick wall facing the public works building. The hearse was in the back driveway, which meant that they weren't having a funeral there tonight. Lucky break.

Earl wished the locks were a little more of a challenge. No one had bothered to install better ones on this old place. Of course, if they had, Earl probably wouldn't be standing here with a broken padlock in his hand, listening to a satisfying soft click and the creak of the door as it opened.

Laurie wheeled Nearly up to the first step. Turning Nearly's chair around, Earl took the handles and then grabbed the frame.

"Can you lift it by the bottom?" he asked Laurie.

"I think so," Laurie said.

"Step at a time," Earl said. Laurie nodded. "On three. One … two … three."

Earl pulled and Laurie lifted and they rolled the wheels onto the next step. The chair alone was almost as heavy as Nearly. Earl took a breath.

"OK, ready? One … two … three."

Nearly started to chuckle. "This is weird, man."

"That's not what I would call it," Earl said. "OK, one more. Ready?"

"Yup," Laurie said.

On three they lifted Nearly to the landing then over the threshold, which seemed like a minor bump, and closed the door behind them.

The last light of the day came in through a small grimy window, filling the room with a slow, dimming glow. Nearly sat and waited as Earl looked at the old system. In the middle of a counter that ran the length of the wall, a microphone sat next to a control panel that was probably eighteen inches square. It wasn't complicated. There was a silver toggle switch for on and off, a few buttons, a couple of faders, and a round, black dial. Earl started to laugh.

"What's funny?" Nearly asked, smiling.

"Do you remember the movie ... aw, heck, what was it called?" Earl shook his head. "There were all sorts of dials and switches, and after the good guys launched the rocket, the thing started smoking and flames came out of it. And you leaned over and said ..."

"Circuit breakers are for wimps." Nearly wheezed as he laughed.

"Really hoping this is built better." Earl's shoulders shook as he chuckled.

Laurie stood on her tiptoes and looked out the window.

"Kinda hard to see but I think that's Aunt Marlene and Mitchell on the corner. I don't see anyone else."

"What're they doing?" Nearly asked.

"Nothing. Just standing on the corner."

Earl toggled the switch up then down a few times. The red light didn't come on. Maybe the bulb was burned out. He listened. Nothing. He followed the cord from the microphone, which was hardwired into the control panel. He crouched down, turned on the flashlight and looked underneath. *Dammit*, he thought. *We got him in here. We just need this thing to work. C'mon.*

Standing up, he put his hands on either side of the panel and closed his eyes to summon whatever he knew about electronics.

"Are you praying?" Nearly asked.

Earl was about to answer when suddenly there was a soft hum and the red light shone like Rudolph's nose at Christmastime.

"Wow," Nearly said looking at Earl.

Laurie stood over by the wall, pointing at the outlet.

"It wasn't plugged in," she said.

"Glad we have you here, Laurie. I was starting to think this might not work," Earl said. He smiled. "I'm surprised no one has cut the electricity to this place." To himself, he added the hope that the speakers were still connected and working. No one seems to pay much attention to old stuff. In this case, Earl hoped that was a good thing.

He didn't want to turn up the dial until Nearly was ready. They would only have ten, perhaps fifteen minutes before someone might show up to put an end to their adventure.

"Uh oh," Laurie said, looking out of the window again. Earl walked over.

"What?"

"Cops," she said nervously, and stepped aside so Earl could look. There was Buddy Wallings in his uniform, chatting with Marlene and Mitchell.

Mitchell was in the middle of telling Marlene about how much he was enjoying being retired from teaching when the police car rolled up. The officer, alone in the car, got out and walked over to them.

"Folks," he said. "Marlene," he added with a nod.

"Hi, Buddy!" Marlene said a little too cheerfully. "Beautiful evening."

Buddy looked around. As if he just figured it out he said, "It sure is."

"Buddy, this is a friend of mine from St. Paul, Mitchell Johansen." The two men shook hands.

"Mitchell, this is Buddy Wallings. He keeps things running safely here in Campbell." Suddenly Marlene was sounding like a character in a Frank Capra movie.

"Nice to meet you, Buddy."

"You related to Earl Johansen?" Buddy asked.

"That's right. I'm his brother. I was on a trip and just stopped by on my way home."

"So, where's Earl?" Buddy asked.

****

"Hey, Earl?" Nearly said. "I'm kinda hot. Does that window open?"

Still looking out the window, Earl was silently willing the officer to move on. He quickly examined the window.

"I think it's painted shut." It didn't matter. There was no way he was going to open the window and have its screeching or squeaking give them away.

"What's happening?" Laurie whispered.

"Nothing. They are all just standing around talking," Earl said in a normal voice. "I don't think you have to whisper. It's not like they're standing at the door."

Laurie nodded.

****

As if it was God's truth, Mitchell said, "Oh, Earl is probably home by now. He was at the VA visiting a friend and I decided to take a walk around my old stomping grounds. Ran into Marlene."

The lie was so well delivered that even Marlene started to believe it. "I haven't seen Mitchell in I don't know how long." she added with a smile.

Buddy smiled too. "Well, I just wanted to make sure you didn't have a car problem or something. You have a nice evening." And with that, Buddy Wallings slid into his police cruiser and rolled off.

"He's gone." Earl turned to Laurie. Nearly looked pale and damp.

"You OK?" Earl asked.

"Sort of hot. I don't think the dinner liked me."

Laurie reached into her backpack. "I have water," she said helpfully, unscrewing the top of a plastic bottle and handing it to him.

"Thanks," Nearly said gratefully. "You're a lifesaver."

Earl nodded a silent form of thank you at Laurie.

"Ready?" he asked when Nearly was done drinking. Nearly nodded.

Earl rolled Nearly up to the counter.

Earl didn't know for sure which of these faders controlled the volume, or if it was the dial. He knew he would need to figure it out quickly. He bumped the faders up about a quarter of the way and turned the dial up a little.

"Laurie, poke your head out and see if you can hear anything. I'm going to tap on the microphone."

Cracking the door open, Laurie stuck her head out. Earl tapped. She pulled her head back in.

"I think I hear something but it isn't very loud."

"OK." Earl eased the faders and the dial up a little more. "Try this."

This time when Laurie brought her head back in she gave him a broad smile and a thumb's up.

"You're on, Nearly," Earl said, moving the microphone closer.

Standing out on the corner, Marlene suddenly heard a voice from out of nowhere say, "Ohhh, OK …"

Mitchell looked at her, his eyebrows raised in surprise.

"Oh my god," he said. "I didn't think this was going to work."

"I think we need to walk down the street a little ways, Mitchell. Let's just walk for a bit."

Nearly cleared his throat. Earl stood next to him.

Everyone in Campbell, Iowa, heard an unfamiliar voice, the voice of Nearly Kelly, a man who had been long overlooked.

"Citizens of Campbell! Heh, heh, heh … that's how they always start it.

Citizens of Campbell. This is ol' Nearly. I don't know a lot of you, but I just wanted to say that it's been nice living here."

Earl looked at him. *It's been nice living here?*

"Della Marsh makes the best burger anywhere. And even though he never liked me, Bob Hansen always poured a good drink."

Earl smiled and scratched the back of his head. Both of these statements were true.

"And when that Vietnamese family came here in '72 and opened up their restaurant, they had a noodle bowl thingy I couldn't get enough of. But somebody set fire to their place and I know who it was and I'm not sorry I slashed all the tires on your trucks." Nearly coughed, wheezing.

Earl sat up a little straighter and looked at him. He had no idea that it was Nearly who had avenged the Tran's loss. It was a well-known secret that Nels Petersen's boy, Karl, back from service, got a couple of his cousins together and after being cut off at Bob's Bar, threw a brick followed by their version of a Molotov cocktail through the front window of Tran's Restaurant.

Nearly continued.

"Thing is, anyplace is nice if you have good friends. Anyway, I haven't had a lot of adventures or anything, but I've sure met some nice people and I have a real good friend. That's really all a guy needs. Now, there's only one thing I have that I really care about, and so now that I have maybe a few hundred witnesses …"

Marlene and Mitchell sat on a bench in the park. They were about two blocks away, public works building in view, listening to Nearly. They sat up straight and watched two patrol cars roll up. Buddy Wallings once again got out in front of the building. Out of the other car came two officers, one holding a rifle, the other with a bullhorn in his hand.

Laurie was looking out of the window and suddenly looked back at Earl with her eyes wide and panic tightening her face. Earl took a look. *Keep talking, Nearly. These three guys are so heavy and out of shape, they couldn't even catch you.* Turning away from the window he looked at Nearly and smiled encouragingly.

"Earl—Earl Johansen—gets my quilt when I'm gone. This is

a quilt my momma made for me and it was supposed to protect me and I think it did a pretty good job."

Buddy and the other officers were striding to the building. Suddenly Buddy put his arm out. They all stopped. Buddy crossed his arms in front of him, cocked his head and listened.

"I want this quilt to go to Earl and I hope it protects him like it did me. So, Wilma, you need to make sure Lars Petersen doesn't get it."

Earl was touched by Nearly's gift, although he flinched when Nearly said "Wilma." But truth was, no one at the VA was likely hearing this broadcast.

"Guess that's about it. You all have a nice evening. This is Nearly—over and out."

Earl flipped the power switch off.

"Great job!" Laurie cheered as she leaned over the back of the wheelchair and hugged Nearly from behind.

"You did it," Earl stated, patting him on the shoulder.

"I did," Nearly said weakly, but smiling. "Earl …" he said.

The next sound was a screech and then an electronically boosted voice: "That's enough—come on out, fellas."

"Just a sec, Nearly." Earl went to the door, opened it and called out, "It's OK! We're coming out. It might take us a while. We have a man in a wheelchair here."

"Earl …" Nearly repeated.

"Don't worry, Nearly. They won't arrest us," Earl said. He noticed Nearly was sweating.

"You don't look so good."

"Yeah. Well, I guess I match anyway. I don't feel so good either."

Laurie held the door open as Earl rolled Nearly out.

"I'll get you back to the VA. You'll be fine."

"My arm hurts."

****

As soon as they emerged from the public works building, the officer with the rifle raised it and got them in his sights.

"Aw, for cryin' out loud, Steve," Buddy said shaking his head. "Lower that thing. Y'got a youngster and two senior citizens, and one of 'em's in a wheelchair!"

The rifle was lowered. The officer shifted his weight from foot to foot, like a teenager caught doing something stupid in front of his friends.

It was officially past dusk now. The officer with the bullhorn shone a flashlight on the trio exiting the building. The damn light was blinding.

"Hey, Buddy." Earl called out, stopping to shield his eyes.

"Earl," Buddy said, walking toward him. "You OK?" When they reached each other, Buddy said, "What the hell, Earl?" Buddy was young enough to be Earl's son.

"No one got hurt." This was all Earl could think of to say. No one got hurt.

"Glad about that," Buddy said. Setting his eyes on Laurie he said, "And who are you?"

Laurie looked at Earl, who nodded at her as if giving permission.

"Laurie Carver. I'm here visiting my great-aunt." Laurie's voice was steady.

"And your great-aunt is?"

"Marlene. Marlene Goodhue."

Buddy rubbed his forehead. "Look, Earl, I know no one got hurt and you're looking on this as a lark, but it's breaking and entering. I'm going to need you to come down and we'll figure something out." He looked at Laurie. "I expect I can release you to your great-aunt. Happy to drop you off."

"Buddy, I need to get Nearly back to the VA. I don't think he's feeling all that well."

"We'll give you a ride too."

In all the years he had lived in Campbell, and with the

variety of pranks he and Nearly had executed, Earl had somehow avoided being charged with anything. He sighed and started pushing Nearly toward the cop cars. His luck had run out. He didn't really care. It was worth it.

"Earl ..." Nearly said with some pain in his voice. "My arm is ..."

Earl stopped pushing. Buddy Wallings, a few steps ahead of Earl turned in time to see Nearly lean over the side of his chair and vomit onto the shoes of the officer with the rifle.

Buddy looked at the bullhorn officer and said sternly, "Get an ambulance. Right now. Go." The officer ran to the car and called in a request for an ambulance.

Kneeling next to Nearly, Earl said, "Hang on, OK? We're getting help."

Nearly grimaced in pain.

Earl had his hand on the armrest of the wheelchair. Getting up from a kneeling position was never easy. Or quick. Before he even tried to move, Nearly put his large hand on Earl's, looked at him and smiled.

"It'll be OK." Earl said. It was a lie. Who the hell knew if it would be OK. It was something people said.

Earl saw Laurie run toward two figures emerging. The streetlight illuminated Mitchell and Marlene. They were gesturing and pointing as they quickly moved toward Earl, Nearly and the police officers.

The ambulance came. Nearly was laid on a stretcher, an oxygen mask covering his nose and mouth. His hair looked even darker against skin that now almost looked the color of the sidewalk.

"I'm gonna ride with him to the hospital," Earl said.

"Sorry, Earl. You need to come with me," Buddy said.

"As soon as Nearly is settled, I'll come to the station. I promise."

"Earl, " Buddy said, "You're not kin."

"I'm his best friend!" Earl protested. "I'm almost the only family he's got!" He lightly touched Buddy's arm. "I'm on his emergency call list at the VA!"

"Sorry. You and I need to go to the station after we drop Ms. Goodhue and her grandniece off. I'm sure the VA will call you if anything happens."

After loitering on the edge of the conversation, Mitchell stepped in.

"I'll take Marlene and Laurie home."

Buddy looked at him for five full seconds. It felt like an eternity. "You weren't in on this." It was a question disguised as a statement.

"No, sir," Mitchell replied with a faint hint of offense. He then looked at his brother and said, "I'll come by the station after I drop them off."

As Mitchell walked toward Marlene and Laurie, Earl watched the ambulance until it turned a corner and the flashing lights disappeared. Buddy was right. The VA would contact him. But it would be too late. Sadness permeated his body with every inhale, every exhale. He got into Buddy Wallings' police car and rested his head against the window.

Earl was not detained long at the station. He agreed to everything Buddy said even though only part of him was listening. As Buddy did the paperwork, he said he would let it go this time provided that Earl do some volunteer work, repairs and such, over at the senior center. He also asked that Earl fix the lock on the public works building's door.

As soon as Buddy said he was free to go, Earl got up, thanked him, but never apologized. Once outside, he looked and didn't see Mitchell. Under a full moon, he walked quickly to the VA. He would not apologize. Not now, not ever. It was the right thing to do. Nearly had his moment and was happy.

When he arrived at the hospital inquiring about Nearly, the

woman at the counter asked him to take a seat. Every minute that passed seemed to confirm what Earl already knew. A doctor finally appeared, a short, older man with a ring of gray hair around his head, the very top of which shined. He said words that Earl had heard on television shows like *ER* and *Chicago Hope: Heart attack ... we did what we could ...*

Earl stood, the doctor's words floating around him. All he could hear was the voice of his heart repeating *Nearly's gone, Nearly's gone, Nearly's gone.*

"Would you care to see him?" the doctor offered.

"Yes. Yes, I would," Earl said softly.

The room was small and quiet. The machines designed to measure and assist now stood dark and mute. Their work was done. Nearly lay on a gurney, a sheet pulled up to his collarbone. Earl stood back, waiting to see if his chest might rise and fall. He walked forward and put his hand on his friend's arm.

"Hey, Nearly," Earl said, tears filling his eyes. "Well, I guess we had a pretty good time, didn't we?" Earl looked at the body in front of him. He had seen this before. The body is just a body. Nearly wasn't here anymore. The only thing left was what had carried him.

"I really don't know what I'll do without you, Nearly. I don't." Earl took his handkerchief from his back pocket and dabbed his eyes. "I'm going to miss you."

Earl heard the door open.

"Sorry. Mr. Johansen?" a nurse said. Earl tried to recover as best he could.

"Yeah. Yes."

"We have Mr. Kelly's things. His directive says they are to go to you. Whenever you're ready, they're over in building three, where he was living."

Where he was living.

"Thank you," Earl said. Placing his handkerchief back in his pocket, Earl took a deep breath and let it out. He patted Nearly's arm for the last time.

"Goodbye, Nearly."

As he left the room, instead of taking a right and heading for the elevator, Earl turned to the left. Strangely compelled to go to the large windows at the end of the hall, he was disappointed to see someone else standing there. It was perhaps another person who was allowing grief to soak into every pore as they looked out into the dark. Earl thought about not going to the window, to let this person have some time. There were other windows. But then he recognized the figure. It was Deborah Kelly. She was leaning a bit on her cane. There were only two people listed on Nearly's emergency contact list. Earl walked up and stood next to her.

"My son," she said sadly without looking at Earl.

The two of them stood side by side watching the night grow deeper.

****

Earl thought it fitting that Evelyn Root was the guardian of the box containing Nearly's worldly goods. The quilt, Nearly's constant companion, lay on top. There was a suitcase that had been packed with Nearly's clothes. The items were listed on a form. Earl signed it and Evelyn gave him a copy. She wasn't in uniform. Later, Earl would wonder why she was there.

"My sympathy for your loss, Mr. Johansen. Mr. Kelly was well liked by the staff here," she said kindly and then added, "He was a good man."

It was past 11:00 by the time Earl returned home. Mitchell had offered to spend the night or have Earl stay with him at the hotel, but Earl declined. It was a kind gesture but making conversation, especially talking about Nearly, seemed impossible. He placed the box on the kitchen table and set the suitcase on the floor. He would go through them tomorrow. The phrase *bone tired* came to him as he lay down on his bed. But as tired as he was, sleep would not come. He closed his eyes and saw Nearly on the gurney. He looked at the clock: *12:04 … 12:50 … 1:20 …*

He got out of bed, filled the small teakettle and put it on a burner that quickly glowed red. If anyone ever gave him a gift, like at Christmastime, it was usually one of three things: a Hickory Farms gift basket, herbal tea or chocolate. Herbal tea and chocolate. That's what people give old folks, he thought. Because he rarely drank tea, he had a cupboard shelf full of it. He may as well have some. There was chamomile, mint, ginger, apple spice, orange spice, peach and one called Sleepytime. Maybe he would try that.

While he waited for the water to boil, he gently touched the quilt that rested on the top of the box. Earl still wasn't sure why Nearly wanted him to have the quilt, but it didn't matter. It was an orphan now. He would take care of it. He picked it up and laid it on the ottoman.

One by one, Earl took out items from the box. There was a blood-red bag containing a few ribbon pins, service in country, basic infantry training—identical twins to the ones Earl had in a box in his bottom dresser drawer. There were several books, including *Huckleberry Finn, Catch-22* and *The Beet Queen*. Earl recognized a pocketknife, made out of some kind of stone and worn shiny from use. He picked up a stack of letters tied with brown twine.

The teakettle whistled, snapping Earl out of his pensive mourning.

Sitting at the table with his tea, he untied the string. He recognized his own handwriting. His eyes again filled with tears. He kept looking through the stack. Most were letters or postcards Earl had written to Nearly, the majority of them during their time in the service. There were also letters from his mother, and a few from someone named Stanley Kaufmann. One of the letters from Stanley Kaufmann had a photograph sticking out of it. It was a picture of a small metal box with a ragged tear in it. *Why in the world would anyone take a picture of that?* Earl wondered. Even though it felt intrusive to look, Earl pulled out the letter.

> *Dear Kelly,*
>> *I made it home OK and I hope you're soon home safe. I got your address from the clerk. You would have thought it was top secret or something. Anyway, here is the photo of your box that saved my life. I hope I can find a way to repay you someday. And if you're ever going to be in New York, I hope you'll let me know. Thanks just isn't enough but it's all I have for now.*
>> *Best, Stan Kaufmann*

Earl smiled. Nearly never said a word about saving anyone. Typical.

As he finished his tea, he placed the items back in the box. On his way to bed, he took the quilt from the ottoman. It was a small quilt, enough to cover a small child or drape over a grown man's shoulders as Nearly had often done. Earl sat on the edge of his bed and put the quilt around his own shoulders. It was comforting. Grabbing at one of the corners, he thought he felt something in the quilt. It was small and hard.

He remembered when Nearly would get anxious, how he would almost knead the quilt in small pushes with his fingers. Earl put the quilt on his lap and did the same.

Nothing. *I'm too tired and I'm imagining stuff now,* he thought. He pressed some more, in different places. *There! What is that?*

There was something inside. But what if Deborah simply ran out of batting and had to use newspaper or something? Looking at the quilt, the art of it, he knew she would not scrimp on this quilt that she was making for her son. Nearly mentioned small pieces of bark that had been sewn in, maybe that's what he was feeling.

Why did Nearly want me to have this?

Earl got up, opened the box and took out the pocketknife.

Returning to his bed, he said, "Sorry about this, Deborah," and carefully cut about four inches of the stitching where he had felt whatever it was. He put his fingers in and pulled out a twenty-dollar bill.

"What the hell?" Earl murmured. He reached in again and grabbed two more twenties. The bills were soft, not crisp, as though they had been through the wash several times. Where was that hard thing he felt? He didn't want to ruin the quilt and needed to find someone who could open it and stitch it back up again.

Earl awoke before 7:00 the next morning, and for a brief moment the world seemed right again. Then a marathon of images came running through, passing in front of his eyes: Nearly in his wheelchair, Nearly making his announcement, Nearly lying still on the gurney. He remembered the pocketknife, the stack of letters, the photo of the little metal box, the quilt and the cash he had pulled out. It was tempting to not move, to stay in bed with his grief, but his curiosity pulled him out.

After Earl called Mitchell and made a lunch date, he showed up at Marlene's house. He had called her as soon as the clock said 8:01, his rule being that calling people before 8:00 in the morning was rude.

"What is this about?" Marlene asked after welcoming Earl and offering him coffee.

"Do you sew?"

As much as she hated to do it, Marlene opened up the quilt, saying things under her breath the whole time: "What beautiful work ... these stitches are amazing ..." When it was open, they stood there looking at twenty-dollar bills that totaled $300.

"What in the world?" Marlene said.

"Well I knew Nearly didn't like banks but this is sort of strange," Earl said.

"What's this?"

A small, square envelope was stuck in a corner. Earl opened it and held up a key with a tag on it.

"Campbell Savings and Trust."

Earl had Nearly's power of attorney and, now that Earl was thinking of it, Nearly had his. He would need to find someone soon to fill that role. He made a mental note to talk to Mitchell about this over lunch. He asked Marlene if she would come with him to the bank.

"Yes, of course, Earl. This is a bit of a mystery. I'll drive," she offered.

Marlene said she would stitch the quilt back together later, perhaps adding a little batting to it. "I can't hand stitch like she did, so a machine will have to do."

After stopping at his house and retrieving the power of attorney document, they went to the bank.

As much as Nearly didn't trust banks, he had a safe-deposit box. Earl knew exactly what his friend was thinking: the box was his, not the bank's and even if the bank went belly-up, the box would still be there. It was a solid thing. Not like a piece of paper that suggested you had some money somewhere. Abel Mercer, the bank officer who was helping Earl, showed him to the room.

"Aren't you coming in?" he asked Marlene.

"This was meant for you, Earl. I'm happy to wait."

"Just let me know when you're finished, Mr. Johansen," Abel said, closing the door.

Earl's memory of what happened next was like walking through clouds or fog. The mix of confusion, sorrow, amazement and amusement made it feel as though he were in a dream, maybe a movie or a play. These kinds of things simply did not happen to him.

In the box was more cash than Earl had ever seen. Wrapped in bundles.

Two letters were on the top. The first, from Cantor, Zwillig and Chase, a law firm in New York, stated that a Mr. Stanley

Leonard Kaufmann had died and left to Mr. Nearly Kelly the sum of $350,000.

Earl sat back in his chair. $350,000! He felt his heart beating not only in his chest but also in his throat. The document was dated January 7, 1984.

The second letter was from Barton Carpenter, a law firm in Des Moines. It was a typed letter that was notarized by the lawyers.

> *I, Nearly Kelly, being of sound mind am leaving all of my stuff—money and everything—to my friend Earl Michael Johansen, 142 Cedar Street, Campbell, Iowa. He already has my power of attorney. Mostly, he's my best friend and I want him to have it. I received a lot of money from Stan Kaufmann. It was nice of him to remember me but I don't need it. There's $100,000 in this box and that goes to Earl. I know he's going to wonder so I'll tell him: I have a savings account here so I put a little in there. I gave the rest to my mom and I don't know what she did with it. Wasn't any of my business as soon as it was hers, just like it isn't any of my business now that this is Earl's.*
>
> *Really hope this works.*

Earl put his head in his hands and wept. His feelings were all over the place. He felt angry that Nearly didn't use the money to make himself more comfortable. He could have had a nice home, and maybe some help later on. He felt overwhelmed by his friend's gift. He wondered whether he could reject it. No, he couldn't. Nearly wanted him to have it. Why didn't he invest it? Earl could only guess.

Alongside the wrapped bills lay something swaddled in a handkerchief. It was the metal box that had saved Stan Kaufmann's life, one of Nearly's mint boxes.

Earl went to the door and asked Abel to come in.

****

The short, energetic summer started to fade. The approaching autumn made the sky bluer, but the days were getting noticeably shorter.

Mitchell went home to St. Paul soon after helping Earl arrange a memorial service for Nearly. After talking her grandmother into letting her stay for the service, Laurie returned to Arizona a week later. Deborah Kelly, having taken her son's ashes, didn't attend. Standing next to her at the hospital was the last time Earl saw her.

Marlene kept in touch with him, inviting him to dinner every now and again. Earl kept his routine of walking to the VA. He would walk there, around the grounds, sit for a few minutes on the bench under the tree where Nearly once told him he'd give Earl a million dollars for a smoke. Some days Earl walked from the VA to the store or Della's.

Returning home from one of these walks, he collected his mail. Al was next door, lying underneath his car, cursing a blue streak.

There was a stiff eight-by-ten envelope. The return address gave Earl the first feeling of happiness he had felt since Nearly died: L. Carver, 15305 Piñon Court, Phoenix, AZ. He took Nearly's pocketknife out from his own hip pocket and opened the envelope. Inside, a letter and a four-by-six photograph of Earl and Nearly.

> *Dear Earl,*
> *I thought you might want this photo. I made*
> *a copy for myself too.*
> *Thank you for being so nice to me while I was*
> *there. I'll never forget my time in Campbell as*
> *long as I live.*
> *I'm so sorry about Nearly and I know you*
> *must miss him. I miss both of you.*

Next time you have one of Della's burgers, think of me!
They are the <u>best</u>!
Don't get too comfortable—one of these days I might
just show up!
Love, Laurie

Earl looked at the photograph and smiled. She had managed to get a good picture of both of them, capturing an image of their friendship. He would have to find a frame for it.

That afternoon, with a light cool breeze blowing through, Earl sat in his chair, feet up and covered with the little quilt that Marlene had repaired so well. He picked up Nearly's copy of *Huckleberry Finn* and it fell open to an often-read page: *We catched fish and talked, and we took a swim now and then to keep off sleepiness. It was kind of solemn, drifting down the big, still river, laying on our backs looking up at the stars, and we didn't ever feel like talking loud, and it warn't often that we laughed—only a little kind of a low chuckle. We had mighty good weather as a general thing, and nothing ever happened to us at all—that night, nor the next, nor the next.*

Earl furrowed his brow. He got up, picked up the photograph and took the shot-up metal box from where it sat on the bookshelf. He missed Nearly.

They would have one more adventure.

He made his way to the phone. When Marlene answered, he said, "Have you ever been to Normandy?"

****

Turtlecub Productions is a booking and management company for singer/songwriter/author Ann Reed.

For more information, please visit:
www.annreed.com

Booking inquiries: annreedmusic@gmail.com

CPSIA information can be obtained
at www.ICGtesting.com
Printed in the USA
FSHW020101160719
60018FS